from
just
cond,
, not
one,
was

hape
fell
right
The
race
ietly
irted

eted
d as

GUNS IN THE DESERT
LAURAN PAINE

LEISURE BOOKS NEW YORK CITY

A LEISURE BOOK ®

October 2003

Published by

Dorchester Publishing Co., Inc.
200 Madison Avenue
New York, NY 10016

ISBN 0-8439-5262-8

Table of Contents

Chapter One

The saga of Caleb Doorn was well known across the wide, savage frontier. In lonely trappers' camps, in the buffalo-chip evening fires of cattle drovers, hide hunters, explorers, soldiers, scouts, even Indian teepees, his story was told, along with the legends of his feats. Still, there were very few of these hardy, courageous souls who had ever seen him, or who would associate the lean, gray-eyed man lounging against a rough log pole before Elmore's general store, in Willow Creek, with the savage, daring fighting man who had been court-martialed at Santa Fé and drummed off the post for insubordination. Caleb Doorn was more than a legend; he was almost a myth. To the whites he was a dread yet fascinating man, lethal with a Kiowa-Apache scalping knife, a long, cumbersome dragoon pistol, or with his fists and booted feet. He had refused to advance against a bristling Comanche village with his unprotected troop of cavalry and had been dismissed from the Army. He wasn't a coward, the whites agreed; he just wouldn't take orders.

By the Indians he was grudgingly admired; he was their kind of fighting man. He fought and thought independently, as a man should, not as a machine, to be ordered here and there regardless of circumstances. They had reason to know him well, for Caleb Doorn's bridle and knife sheath were decorated with little wisps of black, coarse hair. Indian hair.

Among the slightly grinning fraternity of frontiersmen who challenged the Indians, the whites, the soldiers, and even Nature herself, Caleb Doorn was openly agreed with and liked. This reckless, loose brotherhood of marked men was scornful of regimentation, authority, or rule by anything except their own force. They laughed derisively at the soldiers, smiled grimly at the Indians, and out-maneuvered both in an era of lawlessness and violence that kept the far country open only to the daring and able.

Willow Creek was a small trading settlement nestled along a busy little creek fed from the run-off snow waters of the Bitteroot Mountains. It consisted of six log buildings that housed a saloon, a church, Elmore's general store, a massive, well-stocked old trading post, and the several houses that sheltered the permanent residents.

In the spring of the year, the little creek at the edge of Willow Creek blossomed out with wild flowers and emigrant wagons, their dusty, worn sailcloth coverings off-white and stained as the bone-weary, gaunt travelers rested before taking up the trackless battle over the mountains and through the Indian country. Caleb Doorn, fringed buckskin pants and long hunting shirt mildly greasy and stained, leaned indolently against the massive log that helped support the rough board overhang before Elmore's store and watched apathetically as a small band of dirty, creaking wagons pulled frowzily up to the creek. His right hand hung unconsciously beside the sky-blue, beaded scalping-knife with its forked stag handle. At the bottom of the gaudy sheath hung a small circular twig from which dangled three miserly tufts of black, rank hair. On the opposite hip, suspended from the sweat-stained, wide, dark belt that encircled his waist, hung a long-barreled cavalry pistol of Colt's manufacture. The bead-encrusted moccasins finished off the lean-hipped, broad-shouldered figure. The deep-set, calm, and thoughtful gray eyes seemed to be lethargic, but they didn't miss a thing as the ragged travelers down at the creek went about setting up camp.

Caleb Doorn, on first sight, appeared deceptively docile and lazy, but a closer study showed small things that had been unnoticed at first. There was the impassiveness of the eyes; the slight prominence of the rounded jaw and chin; the thin, slightly hawkish nose and the quick, gracefully casual movements of the muscular body. All the things one had heard then began suddenly to take creditable shape, for there was a hard-to-define capability about the man that was at once a warning and a promise that, once aroused, Caleb Doorn would be very dangerous.

The emigrants down at the creek were nothing out of the ordinary. There were scrawny women, gaunt, hollow-cheeked men, and fragile, solemn-faced youngsters. The wagons were battered and scarred and the livestock was thin and dry-eyed with fatigue. Automatically the travelers set up their camp and built small, fragrant fires; spirits arose gradually, and nasal voices sang out to one another. The sounds drifted up to the solid section of Willow Creek, and the general store's proprietor—short, hard-eyed, capable, and dogmatic Si Elmore—came out onto the plank walk built under the overhang of his store and looked callously down at the emigrant camp.

Speaking to no one in particular, he grunted aloud: "More of 'em. Means the pass is open again. Reckon the Oregon and Californy travelers'll be commencin' to come again. That means spring is here." He turned abruptly and saw Doorn watching the camp, too. "Caleb, 'pears to me that Californy oughta be filled up by now."

Doorn tossed a casual, disinterested look at Elmore, grunted audibly, and returned to his speculative watching of the emigrants. His thoughts were somber and shrewd. The nation had recently gone through one of the worst civil wars in history and never had a country been better equipped to

turn its face westward than was America. Eighty percent—
perhaps more—of the emigrants had borne guns through the
bloody conflict, and now, trained and inured to hardship,
they were setting out to conquer and open up their newest
possession, the American West. It wasn't like the Crusades,
he thought, where the warriors rode forth full of pride and
piety, to be butchered by a savage and fanatical foe who knew
all about contemporary fighting. These people were as hard
and as ruthless, at the core, as the land and the Indians they
were pitting themselves against. He straightened up and
walked silently away, balanced on the balls of his feet like a
mountain man. Elmore watched him head toward the camp
along the river with a thoughtful gaze. He shook his head
slightly and went back into the store.

"California?" Doorn watched the man as he spoke.

The suntanned, hawk-faced emigrant looked closely at
Doorn before nodding his head. He guessed the frontiersman
to be a squawman, one of those white men who forsook their
own kind and went Indian. As yet he was new on the frontier,
and beads and buckskin meant only one thing to him:
Indians.

"I reckon. At least we're headin' that way."

Doorn nodded slowly. "You're the first party through so
far this year. You goin' to wait for another train before goin'
on?"

The man snorted derisively. "Hell, no. What fer?"

"Indians."

"Ain't seen any yet that'd scare me, and we've come a long
ways."

Doorn's eyes were sardonic. It was an old story to him; the
plains and forests were full of unknown graves and scattered
bones. Scorn, contempt, and over-confidence had accounted
for more butchery on the trail than ignorance. He let his eyes

wander from the thick, black, low-heeled boots of the emigrant up past his shapeless, dirty woolen britches tucked into the boots. He saw the scarred old cartridge belt, the battered pistol, a butternut shirt of homespun, faded cloth, and the bewhiskered, lined face of a young man whose life had left harshness and hardship etched deeply into every pore. The eyes were good, Doorn decided. Young and brazenly courageous, but good steady eyes.

"You the leader of this train?"

"Yep. Name's Josh Harris." The man looked inquiringly at Doorn. "You a . . . a . . . a native?"

Doorn didn't smile, although he felt like it. The emigrant's fumbling over the insulting term, squawman, wasn't new to him. He nodded and shrugged a little when he answered. "I reckon you could call me that."

His pensive eyes went beyond the younger man to the vast, rolling, endless landscape of primeval wilderness ringed with majestic, purplish mountains in the hazy distance. "At least, I been out here a long time. Long enough to know you'll never get to California with only three, four wagons."

The emigrant smiled slyly. "We got somethin' that'll guarantee our passage among the heathens." Doorn eyed the man carefully and said nothing. Finally the younger man turned and beckoned to Doorn. "Come with me fer a second. I'll show you our passport to Californy."

Together they walked through the motley, ragged camp, with its swirling little gusts of wood smoke, to a wagon, older than the rest, patched and warped. The emigrant jumped lightly to the high poop from the wheel hub, and Caleb followed him. Inside the wagon, among the soiled, pathetic possessions of the young man's family, Doorn saw something that made him catch his breath. Sitting defiantly, arms bound tightly behind her back, large, obsidian eyes blazing scorn and contempt, sat an Indian girl. Doorn looked up quickly to the emigrant who was smiling broadly, wolfishly. The man nodded indifferently toward the girl.

"That there's our passport. Won't no Injuns jump us if they know we'll crack her skull when they do."

Anger leaped into Caleb's face, anger and contempt mixed with a little frustration. For a long moment he didn't speak. The Indian girl was tall and shapely with jet black hair, full, firm lips, and a thin-bridged nose below expressive, haughty eyes. Her clothing was chalky white, beaded buckskin with long, graceful fringes that waved sinuously when she moved. The emigrant was startled when he looked at her. For the first time since her capture, she was smiling slightly, her eyes on Caleb Doorn.

"Where'd you get her?"

"Caught her bathin' in a little creek about twenty miles back." Harris wagged his head slowly and looked balefully at the captive. "Damned heathen. Fought like a cougar. Like to laid out three men afore we got ropes on her."

"You'd better release her."

"Not by a damned sight."

"You're new on the frontier. Her people will attack you for kidnapping her. If you kill her when they attack, they'll kill every man, woman, and child in your party."

Harris shook his head grimly. "They won't attack us while we have her for a hostage."

Doorn sighed in exasperation. "Harris, you're a fool. Indians don't value life like we do. First, they'll attack you for stealing her. Second, they'll fight like demons if you harm her. Alive or dead, you signed your own death warrant when you tied her up."

The emigrant shook his head doggedly, stubbornly. It wasn't in his make-up to concede a point in an argument.

"She stays here, our prisoner."

Doorn turned abruptly toward the handsome Indian girl and knelt beside her. His tongue wrapped itself readily around the guttural, moist dialect of her people, the dreaded Blackfeet. "Who are you?"

"Singing-In-The-Clouds."

"Who is your father?"

"Two Shoots, hereditary chieftain of the Siksika."

"How is it that you are here?"

The girl's black eyes swung venomously toward Josh Harris, who was listening to the unfamiliar Algonquin tongue with uneasiness on his frowning features. "He and four other white men caught me in a creek, taking my bath. They roped me, tied me, and made me their prisoner. The Blackfeet are not at war with the whites, but my family will avenge me." The words were spat out, and there was no mistaking the anger behind them.

Josh Harris shuffled his feet uncomfortably and looked away. Doorn continued squatting in silence for a long time.

Singing-In-The-Clouds turned her handsome face to him, studied his thoughtful features for a moment, and spoke again. "I know you. You are Many Coups, the white man, Caleb Doorn. Called by the Sioux, Silent Outcast." Doorn nodded soberly and remained silent. "You have argued with this outlander. You asked him to release me."

Doorn's head came up. "Do you speak English?"

"Well enough to understand what was said."

"Do these white emigrants know that?"

"No, Many Coups, they do not. I have pretended not to speak their tongue. It is better that way. They say what they wish in front of me. To them I am a dirty heathen." Again the eyes flashed, and Doorn felt an inner thrill at the scorn and rampant fury in their passionate depths. "It is good that I know what they plan. If they are attacked, I am to be offered as a peace token or killed." A sardonic smile showed her even, pearly white teeth. "Whether I live or die, these fools will learn a deadly lesson, will they not?"

Doorn ignored the question. "Singing-In-The-Clouds, if I can get them to set you free, will you repay me by telling your people to let them go across the great hills without trouble?"

"Will you be with them?"

"No. I am waiting at Willow Creek for a white soldier and his troops. I am to guide them south to the land of the Mexicans where there will soon be a war."

"Then I will not try to protect these travelers."

Doorn looked into the uncompromising eyes and saw no mercy. For a long, electric moment, their eyes remained locked. Doorn knew better than to let his gaze falter before an Indian, for the plains people evaluated a man by his courage alone, and a weak, unsteady eye was, to them, a sure sign of cowardice and treachery. Singing-In-The-Clouds suddenly averted her gaze, and a soft, dark blush swept over her. She had heard many stories of this celebrated, morose outcast, and in her heart she recognized that here was a man she could live beside. The thought caused a wave of confusion within her firm, large breasts, and she looked away in half fright, half surprise.

Caleb's voice was low when next he spoke. "Then I must go with them. Singing-In-The-Clouds, they are fools, but they shouldn't be killed because of their ignorance. They will not wait for another train. They will go on alone. Let them go, Singing-In-The-Clouds. They are not going to stop in the land of the Blackfeet. Let them go far beyond your home, to the land that meets the great sea."

Without looking up, she answered stubbornly in a warm voice. "Only if you go with them."

"Then I will go with them. Is it that the brave Blackfeet want me out of their country, too?"

"No, Silent Outcast." In using the Sioux name instead of the Blackfeet name, Singing-In-The-Clouds was acknowledging belief in all the firelight legends she had heard of this strange man. "No, the Blackfeet respect you. But unless you go with these fools, the Blackfeet will not respect them, and their bones will. . . ."

"I go with them, then." Doorn arose abruptly, looked for a long moment into the black eyes of the girl, drew his heavy-handled scalping knife, leaned forward, and slashed the ropes that held her in a quick, fluid movement. Josh Harris leaped forward with a deep growl as the girl flexed her aching arms. Doorn turned on him, his knife held menacingly.

"Don't make it any worse, Harris. This girl goes free."

"Who the hell d'ya think you are, comin' in here and cuttin' our prisoner loose. She. . . ."

Doorn's knife slid noiselessly into its beaded sheath as he interrupted the angry emigrant. "I'm still leaving you a hostage, Harris. I'll go with you myself." The emigrant looked uncertainly from the girl to Doorn.

"What can you do for us? That there Injun girl would be a better trade, in a pinch, than you'd be."

Doorn smiled softly, his eyes watching Harris like a hawk. "Go on up to the Willow Creek store and ask Elmore about me. I reckon he'll figure you got the best of the trade. I'll get you through the Blackfeet if anybody can."

Josh Harris wasn't a quick-tempered man, and the complications that had suddenly engulfed his plan of using the Indian girl for a hostage made him wonder if, after all, the strange white man wasn't right. Without a word he swung around, clambered out of the wagon, and, taking long, purposeful steps, headed toward the Willow Creek general store.

Chapter Two

Doorn helped the girl to the ground, scowled at the startled emigrants, and hustled her toward the village before any of the watching wagoners could collect their wits sufficiently to question him. Once behind Elmore's massive log building, Doorn yanked free the tied reins of a saddleless little sorrel mare, boosted the girl up, and pointed back the way the wagons had come.

"Don't stay on the trail, and don't stop until you get back to the Siksika. Go."

Singing-In-The-Clouds looked down at his bronzed, lean face for a quiet moment, then nodded her head gently. "I owe you something, Silent Outcast."

Caleb managed a crooked little smile. "You owe me nothing. Would any sane man . . . Indian or white . . . try to keep a hawk in a cage, or an oriole hidden, or a beautiful woman a slave?" He shook his head emphatically, answering his own questions in Algonquin. "No. Only a fool would try. Don't blame them for their ignorance, Singing-In-The-Clouds. Pity them for the great store of knowledge they don't possess. Go."

The girl nodded again, took a fleeting, hungry look at his face again, whirled the sorrel mare, and loped off. Caleb Doorn stood slouching in the shade of a massive old cottonwood, watching the lithe, supple body sway rhythmically with the jerky stride of the little mare, lost in thought. That was the finest specimen of an Indian maiden he had ever seen. The fragrant, caressing touch of a vagrant spring zephyr blew over

18

him and the rich luxury of the wild land rode headily on its breath. Doorn sighed, and scratched his ribs lustily.

Evidently Elmore had given Doorn a good send-off. At any rate Josh Harris, deeply impressed, met him when he returned to the emigrants' camp along the creek. "If you'll tell me where your horse is, I'll send a boy for it."

Doorn shook his head. "I don't have one any more."

"You mean you give it to that girl?"

Doorn shrugged. "Wasn't much account, anyway. It was a Cheyenne pony I got when I was ridin' in a Sioux raiding party." He let his eyes roam over the emigrants, who had heard who he was and were surreptitiously studying him. "Maybe I can buy one from you folks."

Harris motioned toward an iron stew pot suspended from a bowed twig. "Come on, let's eat. I haven't had my mornin' meal yet. Hell, I got six, seven good horses. You can have your pick. Be glad to have someone else worry about one of 'em for a while. Anyway, I got all I can do keepin' things runnin' 'thout worryin' about extra horses."

Harris's wife, a youngish woman looking washed-out with a thin-lipped mouth and hard, tired eyes, nodded respectfully at Caleb and handed both men a wooden bowl full of a watery, aromatic stew.

They sat and ate. Caleb hadn't known he was hungry until he ate. "How long you goin' to stay at Willow Creek?"

"Leavin' right after we eat. Only stopped to get three wheels retired anyway. Figger to get across them mountains afore it sets in hot. They say the land on the other side is a reg'lar desert and hotter'n hell 'thout water."

Doorn nodded. "That's right. But this early in the year there ought to be plenty of water for a while yet." He ate slowly, his eyes roaming over the gaunt people, taciturn and tired, and the listless oxen and horses. "You oughta have a week or so to rest up the stock, though, from the looks of things."

Harris frowned into his stew bowl. "I know it, but we can't rest this side of them hills." His face brightened. "We'll lay over a week or two when we get onto the desert. That'll give the critters a chance to pick up. The folks, too."

Doorn watched a bony mare suckling a knobby-kneed little colt frantically hunting for milk that wasn't there. "It's bad to start over the hills with weak stock. There's a lot of bones up there. Not just animals, either, that've been caused by failing critters."

Harris's scowl was coming back. Doorn saw the stubborn set of his jaw and decided to say no more. "Well, we got no choice, Doorn, so I reckon we'll have to try it. Through?" Doorn nodded, and handed the empty bowl to Harris's wife, who quickly sluiced it out and packed it away.

Three men approached Harris, and he nodded to them, pointing a blunt forefinger at Caleb. "Mister Doorn's goin' to guide us over the passes through them mountains yonder." The three men looked gravely at Caleb, who stood up and nodded to them. One of them, a wizened little man of indeterminate years and mousy hair, spat lustily into the dust before he spoke. "Reckon we got a chance, just three wagons?"

Doorn shrugged, and Harris jumped into the breach. "Sure. What's to stop us?"

One of the other men, a big-handed farmer fresh from the Union Army named Jack Bedford, grinned sourly. "You always bein' in a hurry has made us right good time, Josh, but I allow the stock's in pretty hard shape to go a-scalin' them hills up ahead."

Harris's eyes clouded and that peculiar set that Doorn had noticed to his jaw came out. "Jack, we got a goal. We gotta get across them deserts afore summer sets in. You fellers know all that." He shrugged slightly, resignedly. "Sure, the critters'll suffer, but they'll get their rest pretty soon. Now, let's git hitched."

He turned to the unspoken member of the trio, a dark, thick-shouldered man who chewed tobacco with the rhythmic monotony of a cow chewing her cud. "Seth, fetch up that chunky bay horse of mine, will you? Doorn, here, will need it to ride ahead and scout out the trails."

The three men nodded, and walked away. Harris watched them go for a speculative moment, his frown slight but unmistakable. "Always a-worryin', them fellers are."

Storekeeper Elmore, dry-washing his pudgy hands on a flour sack apron, stood beside a tall, graceful Delaware Indian and watched the creaking, lurching wagons start the torturous, gradual climb into the balsam-scented mountains ahead. He wagged his head disapprovingly.

"Now just how in hell's that there sol'jer, Gin'l Kearney, gonna find his way into the Mexican country down south?"

The Delaware, without taking his eyes off the tall, buckskin-clad figure ahead of the lazy dust stirred up by the ponderous wagons, spoke softly. "I take sol'jers. Caleb Doorn tell me, he no back three, five days, I take 'em."

Elmore was a little appeased, but his garrulous features were still on the distant horseman who rode erect, his long rifle balanced across his lap, at the head of the small caravan. "Well, that's better, but I'll be damned if I can figger out Doorn. What're three half-rotten old wagons and a scrubby crew of half-starved clodhoppers to him? Hell, don't he know this time of the year the Injuns are all moving through the mountains, headin' fer their summer huntin' grounds?"

The Delaware looked distastefully at Elmore, and nodded

his head as he turned away. "Caleb Doorn know that, too. He no take pioneers over passes otherwise. He no live in log store. He know things." The Indian was moving away when Elmore turned his indignant eyes on him.

The first day, the little caravan rumbled and groaned over eleven miles of fairly good trail. They could have ground out another mile or two, but Caleb, conscious of the heaving, bony sides of livestock, held them down.

The worst was yet to come. Their night camp was in a little clearing where the charred, scattered remains of old camp-fires were all around them. The emigrants' spirits were higher than they had been in days. Jack Bedford brought a small, thick oaken cask to Harris's cooking fire after everyone had eaten, and the carefully hoarded liquor trickled agreeably down the throats of the men. Massive, slow-thinking, and good-natured Seth Overholt smacked his lips, and spat out his cud of tobacco before he drank. Harris took two large swallows, and Caleb mixed his whisky into his tin cup of hot tea.

The older, dried-up little man, an ex-Texas Confederate cavalryman, held his scraggly beard up with one hand as the fiery liquid burned its way down past his gullet. He set the jug down and turned to Doorn. "You figured keeping that there Injun girl was bad medicine, Josh tells us."

Caleb nodded emphatically. "Stealing her was bad enough. You haven't heard the last of it yet, unless the Black-feet have changed a helluva lot this past year."

The little man ran a dirty hand over the stubble along the sharp edge of his lower jaw. "Might be right at that. I recollect, once, back in Texas, an Injun name of Big Tree gettin' all riled up over something sort of like that. Finally got hung, but he sure lifted a lot of hair afore he was caught up with."

He spread his hands palms up in a deprecatory way. " 'Course them was Comanches."

Doorn smiled slightly. "Comanches are tough, but don't think Northern Cheyennes, Sioux, and Blackfeet aren't just as bad. Fact is, I'd rather fight almost anybody except a riled-up Blackfoot, and that goes for the short, heavy Apaches that live out on the desert you got to cross before you get to California."

The second day put nine more miles between the emigrant train and Willow Creek. The train camped late in the afternoon on a promontory overlooking the pine and fir-dotted off-side of the mountains. Doorn had used the easiest, most-traveled passes, and the weak horses and oxen were holding out better than he had expected. The sun was riding above the horizon when the women built their small cooking fires and the men turned the hobbled horses loose to graze over night on the knee-high, tough buffalo grass that grew among the trees.

Doorn and the four emigrants were sitting in the cool shade of a mammoth old pine tree, resting and content, when Caleb's sunken, brooding eyes, level and indifferent, caught a movement among the trees on the far side of the wagon clearing. He said nothing to the others and watched for a repetition as desultory, relaxed talk among the pioneers went unheeded around him. Again there was a slight, shadowy wisp of movement.

Doorn was certain now. Calmly, almost casually, he broke in on the conversation of the men. "Don't do anything conspicuous, like grabbing a gun or a knife. Just sit as you are."

He looked at Jack Bedford, who was puffing peaceably on a black and stubby little pipe stoked with kinnikinnick tobacco. "Keep right on puffing, Jack." The men were suddenly tense, although they made no overt moves. "In those pines across the clearing I saw some movement. Maybe it's only some varmint."

The old Texan, squint-eyed and sober, grunted dryly. "And then again, it might be a whole passel of redskins, too." He wagged his old head shrewdly. "Danged sly, them redskins. Seen 'em slip up like that many a time back in Texas."

Josh Harris tried to act unconcerned, but Doorn saw the bunching muscles along toward the back of his stubborn jaw. He recognized the sign; Harris was going to be dogmatically stubborn. Caleb decided on a bold front.

He looked directly toward where he had seen the movements and called out: "If our cousins will come out, we will smoke a pipe and eat meat."

At Doorn's shout in Algonquin, the emigrant women looked up, startled and frightened. Fearfully they followed his gaze toward the distant trees. For a long, silent moment there was no answer, then suddenly seven tall, gruesomely painted Indians stepped into plain view. The emigrants gasped, and one of the women couldn't smother the small shriek that arose wildly in her throat.

Doorn didn't bat an eye, but his heart sank within him; the strangers were Sioux warriors, not Blackfeet. They stood fully exposed, their rifles lying casually across the crooks of their arms, scalps dangling from their belts, and their bodies painted, as well as their faces, to indicate a raiding party. Doorn appraised the muscular, stringy bodies and read the painted symbols of the Sioux fighting societies.

He arose and held up his hand, palm outward, the age-old sign of peace, indicating that an open palm held no weapons and plotted no treachery. The Sioux remained motionless. Doorn affected not to notice the slight and walked gracefully forward while the seated emigrants watched, fascinated, their fingers lying close to their pistols and Jack Bedford's pipe emitting a series of gusty little blobs of smoke under the impetus of his badly shaken nerves.

Chapter Three

One of the Sioux, a head taller and ten years younger than Caleb, took two firm steps forward, and stopped. The white man faced him, and their eyes locked. There was a grudging respect in the crossed glances. Both recognized in the other a strong man.

The Sioux spoke, in English, which mildly surprised Doorn. "You not many. Very foolish."

Doorn nodded solemnly. "These emigrants are going far beyond the big desert. I only guide them through the Blackfoot country, over the mountains."

The beady black eyes never flickered. "You, Silent Outcast. I see you twice now." He shook his head in a tight little back-and-forth movement. "No good. Emigrants give us horses and flour."

Caleb's hand was resting casually on the hilt of his heavy knife, and the Sioux let his dark eyes lower meaningfully as the white frontiersman spoke. "We travel in peace. The emigrants' horses are poor and weak. The Sioux don't want them."

"We take 'em and scalps, too, if you no give 'em." He nodded toward the hand on the knife hilt. "No good. I can take knife from you."

Doorn's face was a frozen mask, and his eyes were hooded beneath the drooping lids that sheltered the bright, deadly orbs beneath. "Try it." His voice was very soft, and the other Indians, sensing friction, watched in anticipation.

For a silent moment the tall Sioux looked with confident

irony at the smaller white man, then he shrugged and handed his rifle to one of his companions with several guttural words. The other Sioux formed a small, loose circle.

Doorn read the sign easily. There was going to be a fight. He spoke coldly, without taking his eyes from the warrior. "The emigrants will shoot."

Scorn dripped from the Indian's words. "Let 'em. They will never live to tell of it."

Doorn raised his voice a little, still watching the big Indian. "Harris, I'm going to fight this Injun. Don't shoot until the fight is over. If I lose, you must kill the women first."

The emigrants arose lazily and stood near their wagons where they could see the combatants, leaning on their long rifles. The women and children had miraculously disappeared inside the great rolling hulks that had been their homes for many months.

Harris, lips flat against his teeth, threw his words toward Jack Bedford and the Texan. "Them Injuns are probably only an advance war party. If Doorn loses, we're in fer it."

Bedford and the older man didn't answer. Their eyes were glued on the circling fighters, but the thick-shouldered, tobacco-chewing emigrant with the thick thatch of black, curly hair was half smiling. He was a good rough-and-tumble fighter himself, and the prospect of being killed later was secondary to the tableau now unfolding a few hundred feet away. He shrugged and spoke softly. "Never heard of Injuns comin' right out inter the open and wantin' ter fight, man-to-man, before."

The Texan squinted sagely. "I figger that they're afraid to commence a shootin' attack 'cause they're a war party in their enemies' territory. If the Blackfeet didn't hear the shootin', some whites might, so I sort of allow they want to count a coup on us 'thout no noise." He nodded approvingly. "It'd be quite a war honor if they could slip inter Blackfoot country and collect some white scalps . . . right under the noses of the Blackfeet and whites, alike." The others only half heard him as they watched Caleb and the tall Sioux warrior.

Caleb Doorn was appraising the big Sioux. His adversary was confident of his ability to beat the white man. He moved with a half smile on his face, and his large, black eyes were probing, reading, and measuring his man without the grimness that usually marked an Indian fighter. Doorn turned slowly, standing in the same place, as the Sioux circled him. If he could keep the man moving, he had one slight advantage. The Sioux would have to carry the fight to him. Doorn's massive knife was lying edgewise in his fist while the Sioux' knife, a Green River dagger with a nicked, razor-sharp edge, was held a little forward from the side, like the shiny, sullen tongue of a deadly snake.

The Indian, seeing no immediate opening, began to weary of the by-play. His face had an annoyed, angry flush on it and the half smile had turned down at the lips into a sneer. He was crouching from the waist up, his sinewy legs bent a little at the knees. Doorn knew he would spring in soon, and balanced on his toes. The sun was sinking a little lower all the time, but its light was still a life-giving elixir. The Sioux began an unintelligible dirge, deep in his throat. Doorn suspected it of being a victory song, being sung softly in anticipation, but the words were unfamiliar to him.

When the Indian closed, it was no surprise to Caleb, but he hadn't expected the wary strategy that went with the lunge. The warrior had shot forward like a lightning streak and dropped almost to his knees as he went. Doorn saw, too late, that the Sioux was coming in under his guard. Desperately he tried to lower his knife to meet the attack, but only by dodging wildly backwards and sideways did he avoid receiving the glittering Green River knife in his groin, where it had been calculated to enter his body, ripping upward to disembowel him. Even so, the Sioux knife struck hard against his brass belt buckle, the force of the blow, since he was back-pedaling when it struck, knocking him off-balance, and he went over backwards. The watching Sioux warriors leaned forward eagerly and gave approving cries of encouragement when their tall champion, twisting in his momentum, threw his own body across the white man's prone form.

Caleb squinted hard against the blinding flash of the sunlight and grabbed desperately for the Sioux's knife arm. The man was a squirming, convulsing bundle of steel-like muscles that rippled and writhed as he tried to turn his body enough to straddle the frontiersman. Doorn felt the closeness of the blow as the Sioux aimed a violent thrust at his head. He had rolled frantically away fast enough so that the knife missed his throat by inches and struck, jarringly, into the soft, spongy earth. Before the Sioux could withdraw his blade, Caleb had grabbed the bronzed wrist in an iron grip and fought to bring up his own knife, in part restricted by the rigid body of his enemy.

The smell of the warrior's sweat-drenched body was like death in Caleb's nose, and the straining of his own body made him dizzy. As his knife came up, the Sioux tried to grab Caleb's hand. He missed, spun crazily, and lunged with a dawning desperation for the blade again. Doorn, still beneath the massive form, yanked back his arm, felt the keen blade slice across the Sioux's palm, and heaved with all his strength, throwing the other violently sideways, even as the Indian roared in pain and killing fury as his hot, spurting blood ran gushingly from the torn hand.

Doorn rolled wildly sideways, released the Indian's knife hand, and spun lightly to his feet. He reached up quickly and wiped away the blinding rivulet of sweat that was running into his eyes. The Sioux, mad with anger, reckless and wild, roared an oath and rushed forward, head down and knife arm extended. Caleb was panting and weak from the exertion, but he kept a cool mind.

As the big man came in, Doorn stepped widely to one side and swung his own knife like a club. His aim was faulty, though, and, instead of cutting deeply into the Sioux's skull, only a tiny jar told him that he had struck at all. The Sioux watchers groaned, and the charging Indian, past Caleb, straightened up, dazed, and held an exploratory hand to the side of his head. His left ear was gone, sliced off as neatly and cleanly as though a surgeon had done it.

Bleeding profusely now, hacked and gory, his blood mixing with the awesome, running symbols daubed in black and red and yellow over his shiny, dusky body, the Sioux came in without caution, slashing with the blindness of a doomed man. Caleb tried to dodge away and felt the sullen, burning sensation of a deep cut along his left side, just over the ribs. He jumped backward, so as not to be overwhelmed again by the maddened attack, dropped to one knee, and braced against the rush that brought his enemy in close. Then Caleb's knife, slippery with blood, flashed unerringly inward and upward.

For an awful, deadly quiet moment, the big warrior looked down at Doorn, his knife poised and ready. His face was so close that Caleb could see the little fantail of wrinkles around his squinted eyes. He shuddered, dropped his knife, and his knees buckled as he fell in a writhing heap to the pine-scented earth. A gush of hot, bubbly breath, laden with foam-flecked blood, cascaded from his nose and mouth. Caleb stood poised and ready over his dying adversary, looking at the dumbfounded Sioux warriors. The Indians were glassy-eyed as they watched the disemboweled warrior twitching and gasping on the blood-soaked ground. Slowly they looked up. Doorn, ashen-faced and thin-lipped, was waiting. His fringed hunting shirt was a spectacle of splattered gore, and his wounded side was dripping warm blood that mixed on the earth with the congealing little pools of the dying man's blood.

Without a word, three of the remaining warriors went forward and lifted their fallen comrade and carried him stoically out of the little glen. The other Sioux fighting men were staring bitterly at the white man. They eventually turned and followed their companions into the gloom of the shadowy forest. Caleb turned, and walked wearily back to the emigrants, expecting to feel the tearing agony of a rifle ball in his back any second, but almost too tired and spent to care.

Night spread its somber blanket of darkness over the fearful little emigrant camp. Caleb had explained to the settlers that Indians, in general, would not fight at night, believing that a warrior killed in the dark would never find his way into the hereafter. However, aching in every joint, he joined the others in a hidden cordon, scattered among the bushes and trees outside the wagon encampment site, where each of the four men kept a wide-eyed, sleepless vigil, lest the Sioux should return for vengeance.

Dawn was an interminable surcease that seemed forever in coming. The emigrants, half afraid to move, slipped back to the wagons with the first glow of pink off in the east. Their women and children, white-faced and shaking, were set to barricading the wagons. There was a fresh, saintly fragrance in the air when the first rifle shot came spanking down the wind to them. Doorn, sore and stiff, his wounded side a searing, fire-like burden with every breath, told the others in curt, clipped sentences, that yesterday had been a picnic. Today—this morning, in fact—was the deciding moment for them all. He minced no words when he told them that only a miracle would see them ever leave the mountains alive, and he had never seen a miracle in his life.

Grimly the men set the women to loading rifles while they peered cautiously from under the great sailcloth shrouds where they were secured to the high, gracefully curving wagon boxes. No movement met their slitted eyes. No birds sang; no crickets croaked in their hidden, grassy world. Doorn shook his head. "They're out there, all right. Stand ready, boys. They've got to do this in a hurry and they know it. The noise of rifle shots will carry a long way."

He had scarcely stopped speaking when a furious fusillade sprang up, not three hundred feet from the wagons. Splinters flew as the balls riddled the wooden sides. Jack Bedford thrust his rifle quickly out of a wagon, sighted, and fired. He swore and reached for another rifle. Caleb saw two flitting shapes, and methodically threw two rapid shots from his Colt at them. An Indian screamed exultantly, and the emigrants shuddered. The old Texan fired, swore, exchanged rifles, and fired again. This time there was a harsh smile on his face. An attacking Sioux toppled grotesquely out of the crotch of a tree and hit the ground with a sodden, dull *thud*.

Chapter Four

They were coming in now, throwing caution to the winds, anxious to finish it off and disappear with their trophies, and to exact every last drop of revenge. Caleb saw them charging through the trees, four hate-maddened, powerful, painted Indians, running recklessly in zigzag lines that made accurate rifle fire impossible. Caleb shouted to the others and threw himself flat, cocking his long barreled six-gun.

Josh Harris swore furiously. "A firebrand!"

Caleb hadn't seen it. One of the Sioux tossed a big pitch firebrand in a large, drooping arc. It fell squarely on the sagging top of the wagon they were all crouching in, and the dry, half-rotten, old sailcloth caught like tinder. He felt the sting of molten pitch and cloth as the fire raged overhead and leaped to his feet. "Run for it. Try to get to the next wagon, up ahead." He swung to Harris. "Get the women and kids out of here. We'll try to cover them. Hurry!"

It was useless, and Caleb knew it. The besiegers were in the trees on the far side of the clearing now, as they had planned to be, crouching, their rifles steady and waiting for the first emigrant to make a break from the fiery arc of the burning wagon. Caleb's heart sank and he muttered a rusty, half-forgotten prayer as the old Texan's wife, a thin, sparse woman, white-faced and resolute, leaped awkwardly from the wagon. Three half-crazed youngsters followed the old woman. She ran with desperate agility toward the wagon ahead, keeping her own body between the Indians and the children. The horror-stricken emigrants were firing franti-

cally into the trees where they knew the Indians were hiding
—firing without a target, but with the hope that their volley
might spoil the Sioux' aim.

The thunderous roar of guns was deafening and the acrid,
eye-stinging fumes from the spent ammunition made a sulphurous odor that encompassed the emigrant camp and its
grassy, little clearing. The old woman was shoving the children into the wagon when Caleb saw her sag. His throat was
tight. She jerked spasmodically twice more, as leaden balls
ripped and plowed into her flesh. She sagged, tried to force
herself upright, then collapsed.

A wild, terrifying shriek split the air and made Doorn jump
involuntarily. He swung around just in time to see the old
Texan, a Bowie knife in one hand and his old cap and ball
pistol in the other, leap out of the wagon. Instead of running
toward the other wagon, he screamed wild, blasphemous
curses in a shrill, ragged voice and charged across the little
meadow toward the woods where the hidden Sioux were
watching. The others in the wagon dared not fire as long as
the old man was running forward in their line of fire. A
breathtaking moment of suspense overhung the battle-
ground. It lasted a short few seconds, then a Sioux rifle,
hidden and muted by the dense foliage, coughed its deadly
message. The old Texan missed his footing, stumbled, recovered his balance, and charged on, his pistol spitting fire
and smoke. Again a Sioux rifle roared, and this time the little
old man fell limply, his feet beating a tiny tattoo out in the tall
grass, the rest of his body lying hidden in the thick underbrush.

The little tragedy was over and the rifles began their
furious cannonade again. Josh Harris and Jack Bedford ran
with the rest of the emigrant women and children for the next
wagon as the fire ate lividly into what remained of the other

one. Caleb and the tobacco-chewing, thick-shouldered emigrant dodged and streaked after the others. Caleb threw himself into the wagon as a bullet struck inches behind him. He turned quickly and grabbed the sweaty shirt of the other man and yanked with all his might. The emigrant was almost into the enclosure of pitted, scarred wood when a strange, horrified look spread over his face and, with an unexpected impetus, he lunged far over Caleb's crouching form and fell among the débris. Caleb helped him into a crouching position before he noticed the thin trickle of blood running down the man's trousers.

"Hard hit?"

His jaws working wildly on the mangled cud of tobacco, the man looked up at Caleb in disbelief. "Look," he said incredulously, pointing to his posterior. "Shot plumb through the rear end."

Caleb felt no humor right then. The Sioux ball had penetrated the man's buttocks from side to side. It wasn't for a long time afterward that the humor of the incredulous emigrant and his half-embarrassed, half-painful grimace of pain struck his funny bone. "Set still and take it easy, if you can."

The man's eyes crinkled a little through the grime of his lined, powder-grimed face. "I can take it easy, I reckon. But, by Gawd, it'll be a danged long time afore I do any sittin'."

The Sioux firing had ceased, and Caleb guessed the reason. They were circling around, getting ready to throw another firebrand. He cautioned the others, and the silence was even worse than the bedlam of the attack. Suddenly a wild, deep-throated scream broke across the cool mountain meadow. A crazy patchwork of erratic rifle fire blossomed out behind the wagons. It swelled and roared into a deafening crescendo. The emigrants turned white faces to one another.

Doorn felt dread and shattered hope in his bowels. "Must

35

be the rest of their war party."

Josh Harris, his face working like a man demented, jumped to his feet. "If we gotta die, let's do it standin' up, not hidin' in here like a passel of mice."

Caleb, being next to him, heard every word, but the others couldn't make out what he was screaming over the crashing, roaring medley of gunfire that sent bullets all around them with an abandon that was overwhelming. He saw the madness in Harris's eyes and lashed out with his fist. Harris collapsed in a heap among the broken furniture and sweaty bodies of his comrades.

As suddenly as it started, the gunfire stopped. A pall of awful silence hung over the crouched, bleary-eyed emigrants as they huddled low in the old Conestoga. Caleb risked a hazardous peek, and his eyes widened. Systematically scalping fallen Indians were other Indians! A dawning realization swept over him. He took a better look, recognized the clothing and the painted symbols of the Blackfeet, and hurried out of the wagon, followed by stunned, dizzy, and completely exhausted emigrants. Josh Harris, having come to, was among them.

While Caleb Doorn, a wraith in fringed, smoke-tanned buckskin, blood-spattered and grim, stood watching the Blackfeet among the pathetic little clutch of dazed emigrants, the Indians arose from their grisly chore and stood in silent wariness. Caleb let his gaze roam from the scorched, churned-up clearing with its rank odor and bullet-scarred trees to the fringes of the forest all around the wagons. There were Indians everywhere. If they came for war, resistance would be useless and brief.

He licked his chapped lips, and turned his bloodshot eyes to Josh Harris. "They're Blackfeet."

"War party?"

"I reckon. They're painted and armed for war, but I see women among them, too, which isn't customary."

"Sure's a helluva lot of 'em."

Doorn nodded wearily. "Biggest war party I ever saw. They must've been slippin' up on us when they ran into what was left of those Sioux. That'd account for all that shootin' back among the trees." He nodded thoughtfully. "They sure made quick work of 'em."

Harris, his jaw slack and tired, nodded glumly. "Yeah, well, what do we do now?"

Doorn shrugged. "I'll go council with 'em." He drew himself erect with an effort.

Josh Harris laid a restraining hand on his sleeve, hard and rank with caked blood. "No fightin'. If they're gonna fight, then by Gawd, we'll all fight this time. You aren't in no shape. . . ."

Doorn shrugged off the hand. "Let's wait and see."

He walked slowly across the bruised and broken grass toward the largest gathering of Blackfeet, who were standing looking down at the dead Texan. They watched him come up with impassive faces. Caleb raised his arm and held his hand, palm outward, toward them. One of the Blackfeet, an old man with a deeply lined, scarred face and badly healed broken nose, returned the salute while the others remained stolidly motionless.

Caleb's throat was dry and his voice sounded oddly harsh in his own ears when he spoke. "It is well my brothers came when they did."

The older man grunted wryly, a flicker of a bitter smile on his face. "It is better yet that Silent Outcast made the emigrants release my daughter, Singing-In-The-Clouds."

Doorn grunted. "You are Two Shoots?"

"Yes. And I know you. Silent Outcast."

There was a moment of awkward silence, then Doorn motioned to a scalped, gory-skulled Sioux lying in the brush nearby. "Sioux raiding party?"

Two Shoots was not to be put aside. He ignored Doorn's remark, his frosty old eyes unblinkingly on Caleb. "Singing-In-The-Clouds said you gave her your horse?"

Doorn flushed uncomfortably. He didn't want to discuss the girl or her enforced release from the emigrants. It was thin ice with the hot-tempered, vengeful-minded Blackfeet. He made a wry face. "It would have been a long walk back to the Siksika."

His tart tone amused Two Shoots, although his face remained saturninely half smiling. "I will give you many horses for that favor."

Caleb's face burned a quick red. "Dammit. I don't want your horses. Keep 'em. The emigrants are fools. They thought by keeping Singing-In-The-Clouds that no Indians would attack them."

"Did they think she could save them from the Sioux?"

"I told you they are fools. One Western Indian looks like another to them."

Two Shoots let his mud-colored eyes glide over Doorn's shoulder to rest balefully on the little crowd of rigid, silent emigrants huddled near their wagons. He jutted his chin toward them and spoke without taking his brooding stare from them. "They travel westward, on the great trail?"

"Yes. To the land that meets the sea."

"It is well. Such fools would not live long in the land of the Blackfeet." He turned back to Doorn. "We were following your trail. I wanted to give you horses and frighten these fools for my daughter." He turned to a lean, stalwart man behind him. "Take your fighting men and guide these white fools beyond our land. Take them out onto the big desert and leave

38

them there." His battle-scarred face swung back to Caleb and his eyes were intense and watchful. "You, Silent Outcast, will return to the Siksika with me."

Doorn frowned. "Why?"

Two Shoots held out his hand, palm upward and open. "Because Singing-In-The-Clouds wishes it."

Doorn looked into the fierce eyes for a long, thoughtful moment and the vision of a tall, graceful olive-skinned, black-eyed beauty floated across his inner vision. It was an apparition of pure loveliness that had a warm, generous smile hovering over the full red lips, a fantasy that was designed to take the hollow loneliness out of a wilderness man's solitary, brooding life. Slowly his hand came up and lay for a fleeting, warm second over the open palm of Two Shoots. "You will see that the emigrants are taken safely onto their trail?"

"Yes."

"I come with you to the Siksika, to Singing-In-The-Clouds."

Two Shoots's battered features spread into a toothy, strong smile and he nodded his head wisely. "Had I returned without you, I might have become an emigrant, too. It is well."

Caleb smiled for the first time in a long while, and the two men walked into the forest, toward the painted, pastoral horse herd, side-by-side.

Guns in the Desert

Chapter One

There was a hard yellow sun shining. The sky was faded blue and ragged at its farthest corners. It was one of those late summer days when something has to happen. It was dehydratingly hot, harshly yellow, and down where the desert ran endlessly wide and deep from Singing Springs there was a misty haze almost like the ground-smoke from a forest fire.

There was a feeling in the air, a scent maybe, but whatever it was, men didn't mistake it. A faint brimstone-like odor. At Odell's rooming house which lay two doors north of Hilton's Cinch-Up Saloon, Paul Kandelin told Jess Wright that, if it wasn't hot enough to melt the ears off a brass monkey, he didn't know a hot day when he saw one. And Jess came right back with one of those wrinkle-nosed looks and acted like he was sniffing the air as he said: "Trouble, Paul. Trouble's comin' sure as I'm born. I can smell it."

Paul remembered that for a long time. He'd repeat it *verbatim:* "Trouble's comin' sure as I'm born. I can smell it." But Jess's observation, like every similar observation since the beginning of time, didn't have any punch left to it after the trouble came, because by then everyone knew about the trouble and one man's whistling in the wind didn't mean much.

Except for that jumpy feeling folks had in Singing Springs that day, which was a little like having pink worms for nerves that wouldn't lie still, that kept writhing and twisting, outwardly everyone acted about as they'd always acted. Summer days at Singing Springs were always fierce. Summer days in any part of New Mexico, even in the high country, were fierce. New Mexico was just one of those places where the summer sun rolled out layers upon layers of wilting heat, then rode aloofly back and forth across a pale-burning sky making sure no clouds came up to cool things. The folks who'd lived in New Mexico for any length of time knew how it was—how it *always* was—and, if they had the sense God gave a lizard, they also knew how to live with the heat.

Paul Kandelin should've known how to mop off sweat and move slowly and stay inside during the hottest part of the day, because Paul had been at Singing Springs for six years now as a freight and stage office manager. But some people have a knack for living and learning, and some, like Paul Kandelin, have a knack for just living.

Jess Wright on the other hand was a different breed of man. Jess was like a piece of jerky; his hide was burnt nearly black, and it was stretched taut over a big, old, raw-boned frame strung out for more than six feet in height. Jess didn't pack an ounce of surplus weight, his face had the perpetually shrewd and assessing squint of a lifelong desert-country man, and, although he was rarely without a cud of chewing tobacco pouched low in his left cheek, no one ever saw Jess make any chewing motions, or for that matter they never saw him expectorate. A man like Sheriff Jess Wright knew the value of saliva, or water in any form, and the hotter it got, the slower Jess got to moving and the quieter he became, because Jess Wright was one of those men who lived *and* learned.

You never saw an Indian or a Mexican or a rattler or a lizard or a Gila monster move quickly during the hot time of year. Sometimes a desert tortoise would require five or six days just to move twenty feet. Jess never got *that* slow, but still there was a similarity.

Pete Odell once said Sheriff Wright of Yaqui County was

the only skinny feller he'd ever seen who'd stand in one place so long that, when he finally moved, his shadow remained behind. Pete was a kind of a card. He'd make jokes that were genuinely funny when it was even too hot to laugh. He was a rough man with big, scarred fists and a sideward sly way of shooting a look from under his bushy eyebrows that was a signal that he'd just thought of something funny. There was a rumor that Pete had once been a famous outlaw, and a close look at Pete Odell gave one the definite feeling that this could be true, whether it actually was or not, because, although he now ran a rooming house and was a sort of mother hen to stage travelers and other strays who arrived in Singing Springs, Pete had that cagey, knowledgeable look to him. Like Buster Hilton who owned and operated the Cinch-Up Saloon, though, folks around the Singing Springs country accepted Pete Odell for what he *now* was, not for what he'd probably been ten, fifteen years earlier. Although with Hilton it was different. Folks *knew* what he'd been. There'd been a big hullabaloo years back when Buster had been shot off his horse in the roadway over in Coffeyville, Kansas during a daring, daylight stage hold-up. Buster's beetle-browed, dark, scarred visage had been on the front page of every newspaper in the West for that one, and afterward, even six years later when he'd been released from Leavenworth Penitentiary, he'd made the same papers all over again just because he'd been turned loose.

Singing Springs was that kind of a town. It had its respectable element. In fact, Odell and Hilton and Kandelin and Jess Wright were all respectable men. Middle-aged men usually are respectable, regardless of what they'd been ten, fifteen years before. It seems to be one of the obligations of middle age to cut out the fancy footwork and settle down, and settling down just naturally means turning respectable. Anyway, as Jess had often observed, it was just too damned hot in New Mexico in the summertime for middle-aged men to get all in a sweat over anything—stages, bullion shipments, banks, fat cattle, or breedy horses—so, although the old temptation may occasionally rise up to prick an old owlhooter, the wisdom of the years tells him plain out that the risks just don't equal up to the hard work.

Singing Springs lay sixty miles north of the Mexican line. In earlier times it had been on the route of contraband runners going and coming—going into Mexico with guns, coming out of Mexico with raw gold, usually stolen. But those days were pretty well gone now. True rustlers still operated in the border country, but gunrunners belonged to another generation. Mostly now Singing Springs saw few real badmen, and furthermore, as Jess said, the outlaws of these days were a far cry from the outlaws of fifteen years back. Nowadays they rode quietly into a town, put up at Odell's place, bought a bath, a shave, a big supper, had a few belts of Hilton's Taos lightning, and maybe smoked a cigar or two while loafing over at Brigham Pruett's saddle shop, then went on their way.

"Not like they used to hit a town. They'd come in out of the late-day sun all dusty and devilish. They'd tie up and walk sort of stiff-legged down the center of the road without sayin' anything, just sort of boldly lookin' at the town and softly smilin' like they wanted folks to know who an' what they were, and dared any livin' man with a gun to do a damned thing about it. An' if no one choused 'em, or, if they was just goin' on through, there was no trouble. But, hell, those days are gone." Well, Jess was right up to a point. Where he was wrong was where it hurt. Those days weren't really gone; they were just getting fewer and farther between.

He was over at Pruett's shop. It was Friday morning, hot

as the hubs of hell without a breath of air stirring and with that hazy summertime mist lying over the southward land. There were a few of the roundabout cowmen in town, mostly with wagons and their womenfolk for the weekly shopping, and, if Jess or anyone else had been asked to designate a typical midsummer day at Singing Springs, New Mexico Territory, they'd have named this particular day.

A young stranger had just ridden in from the south. What made him noticeable in shirt-sleeved Singing Springs was the fact that, although he wore a black shirt open at the throat, which was normal enough, he also wore a fawn-colored lightweight coat that fell from broad shoulders to just below his gun belt. No one ever wore a coat in Singing Springs in the summertime, not even early in the pleasantly cool mornings.

Jess saw him through the window of Pruett's saddlery and commented about that coat. Brigham Pruett, a shock-headed big burly man who rarely had much to say, looked and shrugged and went on wetting down a fresh-cut seating leather he was going to shape across a saddletree. If that stranger wanted to wear his fawn-colored coat when it was approaching a hundred degrees Fahrenheit outside, it was fine with him.

The stranger led his horse over to Charley Miflin's shoeing shop and left him. He stood outside in the bright shade of an overhang and made a slow cigarette while he studied Singing Springs. While he lit up and studied the town, Jess Wright also discreetly studied *him*.

Angie Miflin went past with her pa's dinner pail and Fawn-Colored-Coat turned gradually from the waist to include pretty Angie in his study. Jess's lips pulled down a little. Not that he blamed the stranger at all for admiring Angie at all. She was the handsomest girl between Teocali, Mexico and the Missouri River. It was just that Angie belonged to Singing Springs and that lanky, leaned-down stranger out there didn't and, in Jess's eyes, never would.

Across the way at the general store two cowboys met who evidently hadn't seen each other in several weeks and boisterously called back and forth. This diverted Jess's attention for a moment, and, when he looked back, Fawn-Colored-Coat was sauntering on up toward Buster Hilton's saloon. Then an odd thing happened. Angie came stepping forth from her father's smithy, stopped, and put a very deliberately assessing gaze upon the tall, youthful stranger, as though she'd also noticed him. Jess saw her face plainly; it was bright with quick, sure interest and strong curiosity. He made a disapproving, clucking sound, and started on over to the doorway where he halted, leaning against warped wood, and watched those two.

Fawn-Colored-Coat disappeared into the Cinch-Up without once glancing back. Angie, her spun-gold hair flashing sunlight, tilted her head and started northward up the overhang-shaded plank walk. Now she looked miffed about something. Jess shook his head. Women!

"Hey," growled Brigham Pruett from back in the cool, shadowy interior of his shop.

Jess turned.

"You figure she's goin' to go on bein' Charley's cook an' bottle washer all her life?"

Jess blinked.

Pruett raised a skiving tool and pointed with it at his front window as he said: "Seventeen dollars that window cost me. You figure I got a big one just because I need sunlight in here? Like hell. That there's my hobby. Bein' a bachelor . . . like you . . . I need one. I watch folks." Pruett lowered the skiving tool and gave Jess one of his very rare, toothless grins. "Been watchin' young Angie grow up for a couple of years. Been also watchin' how the range riders been beginnin' to take notice. A feller who works alone like I do sees a lot of things, Sheriff." Pruett's dour eyes crinkled a little. "You'd be surprised."

Jess kept watching the saddle and harness maker. Pruett had arrived in Singing Springs two years before with all his worldly goods in a two-wheeled cart drawn by a rump-sprung old ring-boned mare. He was a good saddle and harness man, and Singing Springs had needed one. Pruett had set up shop and had been as busy as a cat in a box of shavings ever since. But he was a taciturn man who kept entirely to himself. No one knew anything about Brigham Pruett. He did his work well, charged fair prices, and minded his own business. You couldn't ask any more than that of any man. He was a thickly made man with a great thatch of unruly, curly graying hair and had always struck Jess Wright as a man who'd make a staunch friend and an implacable enemy. He lived over at the rooming house, as Jess also did, ate at the adjoining Mexican's café, and that was about all Jess or anyone else knew about him, which was why Jess kept gazing at him now. He'd never given a thought to what might be going on inside Brigham Pruett's head—like studying folks through his saddle shop front window. Well, there were all kinds of men in this world, and, if you didn't go around rubbing their fur the wrong way, usually they were tractable and pleasant enough.

Jess shrugged. "I wasn't thinkin' about her growin' up," he said. "I was thinkin' about . . . hell, let it go."

Pruett nodded. "I know. But one of these days one of 'em'll ride into town, smile with the sun in his eyes an' the whistlin' wind in his laugh, an' she'll ride off with him. Nature made it that way. Maybe you don't approve. Maybe I don't, either. But that's the way it is, Sheriff."

Chapter Two

At eleven o'clock Jess Wright went across to the Mexican's place to eat. It was a little early, but that was one of the basic differences between town men and country men—one ate according to the watch in his pocket, and the other ate according to the pangs of hunger in his stomach. Jess didn't carry a pocket watch.

The noon stage came in, early for a change, disgorged three passengers, changed horses, picked up its fresh whip, and went dustily careening on southward. This happened every day, and, while strangers alighting aroused mild interest, unless they were handsome females, which they rarely ever were, folks soon lost interest, all but Pete Odell anyway. Pete had professional reasons for being interested. His rooms ranged in price from two bits a night to a dollar a night. He seldom got anyone he could charge a dollar, but Pete was an incurable optimist and hopefully scanned every fresh arrival in Singing Springs.

This time, though, like most other times, the three new arrivals at Singing Springs were two-bit customers. One was a man on foot, lugging his war bag and his saddle. Another was a hardware drummer in town to peddle his wares at the general store, if he was lucky. The third passenger was a thin-lipped man with a tugged-forward hat who could've been a cowman, an Army sutler, a doctor, a lawyer, or a bank robber. He blended into the country as only men can who belong. He didn't waste a second glance upon the town but headed straight for the Mexican's café, and, as Jess Wright walked out, he walked in.

The sun was hanging up there, an immense, lemon-yellow obelisk, and Singing Springs began to wilt. Yonder, up in front of Hilton's saloon, Fawn-Colored-Coat was leaning upon an upright post of the overhang. He'd evidently had his few drinks inside and now was content, like most desert-wise folks, just to lean somewhere, patiently motionless and quiet.

Jess heard horses coming. It was too hot to be running animals, but these horses were rocketing right along. The only time local men roweled their animals in this kind of weather was when there was a fire on the range, or a baby was coming into the world, or someone had met with an accident. He turned, picking up that oncoming rush of raw sound, and gazed westward where the horsemen would come sweeping around the north-westward stores and houses. In that direction he saw the lazy dust hanging where these men had sped along.

Then they whipped around onto the main thoroughfare, leaning with their mounts, two of them, strangers to Jess, dressed in faded pants and sweat-limp shirts of range riders, their hats layered over with dust and their carbine boots slung forward so that the rifle butts jutted upward beside the saddle swells, which was the handy way to carry Winchesters for a quick yank and tug.

Over in front of Pruett's saddle and harness shop an old man was dozing on a bench. Up in front of the Cinch-Up that youthful, tall, and coated stranger stood like he was carved out of wood. Jess himself was down in front of the Mexican's café. Otherwise, the roadway was empty of people.

There were wagons with drooping teams here, and a scattering of saddle animals stood hip-shot in the breathless heat at the store front tie racks. It was a typical drowsy Friday morning, except for the dust and rush of those two strangers.

51

They spun in over at the saloon, dismounted, and looped their reins. Jess watched them. That feeling he'd had earlier, when he'd been loafing with Paul Kandelin, came back again. Trouble.

It was an alien smell in the hot atmosphere. It was a lump behind a man's belt. It was a jangling at the ends of a man's nerves. He sucked his teeth, watched the brace of strangers, and spat into the dust of the roadway. When a man got to be thirty-five he imagined things. Those two were just a pair of travelers passing through who'd spotted a town and couldn't wait to wet their whistles. Then one of them stepped out into the roadway with his head tilted, with his bold glance sweeping like a raw challenge up and down, across and back, and placed both hands upon his hips, and Jess stopped sucking his teeth. *Well, here it is . . . trouble.*

The other one also turned his back upon the horses at the rack and gazed upon Singing Springs as though it was a fat old cowering man with his pockets full of gold.

Over in front of the saddle and harness shop that dozing oldster suddenly came wide awake. No one had made a sound, but something had touched that old man's sensibilities and he sprang his watery eyes wide open, saw those two bronzed young two-legged wolves over there, got up, and fled around the corner of the building. That's how solidly and swiftly the atmosphere could change, could flash warnings.

Jess spat into the roadway dust again, hitched at his shell belt, and resignedly started walking northward. The best way to winnow the meanness out of a bear cub was to extract his teeth before he got set to bite, and the easiest way to do this cost exactly thirty cents—you bought them both a drink and stood at the bar having one with them. They talked, looking restless and ready to spring, and you listened, looking careful and patient, waiting for the liquor to make them slightly leaden.

They saw him coming, saw the dull glow of his metal badge. One of them said something from the edge of his mouth, then they both turned. There was the dull flash of steady fire in their eyes and a rusty splash of hot red in their cheeks. The one farthest out in the roadway showed his teeth. They were very white and very even. He was a handsome man, no more than twenty years old, if he was that. But it was there for Jess Wright to see: the tied-down blue-black gun riding in its greased holster, the wild expression, and the brilliant eyes. Hellions came in many shapes and sizes, but they all bore the same stamp.

Jess halted upon the plank walk's edge, gazing at those two. "Hot," he said quietly. "Even for so early in the day, it's damned hot."

The one closest in chuckled. It was a rich, pleasant sound, but it didn't match the yeasty flash of this one's dark blue eyes. "Yeah, it's hot, Sheriff. An' it just might get a lot hotter."

The meaning was clear enough, but Jess ignored it. He'd spotted the one out there in the center of the roadway as the leader. To this one he said: "You're new to Singin' Springs, boys. We got a custom here . . . Singin' Springs stands the first drinks."

The one with those dark blue eyes chuckled again. The one farther out didn't look away from Sheriff Wright, but his smile stayed up, hooked upon the tilted-up corners of his wide mouth. He was appraising Jess, reaching for some conclusions about that long-legged, lean, nut-brown older man facing him. Finally he said—"That's right neighborly."—and there was the homely sound of back-country Texas in his voice. "Only we didn't come to Singin' Springs for a drink,

53

Sheriff. No, sir, we been a long time on the trail. We come for a little fun."

"There's poker and pedro and fan-tan, an' there's liquor," spieled off Jess. "But that's about the size of it, boys. This isn't Tucumcari or Santa Fé or Albuquerque."

The one out in the roadway looked around and back again, still with his reckless, loose, and easy smile. "It'll do, Sheriff, it'll do. It's *got* to do, y'see, because them other places . . . well . . . you know how it is, Sheriff, we just don't feel right in them other places."

With his face bland to conceal the congealing thoughts behind it about these two, Jess nodded gently and said: "I'll stand the first round. The saloon's right behind you."

If they were outlaws, as they seemed to want him to believe, then Jess was willing to accept that. But they were neither of them old enough to have been at it very long. The danger from this kind, though, was that they neglected to use the caution one invariably found in older gunmen. These two were the young pups of the breed who challenged every shadow; because they were totally unpredictable, this kind was the most dangerous. Older gunmen weighed all chances, all risks. This kind didn't; they started shooting first and hoped they could get clear afterward.

"Well, now, Sheriff," drawled that one out in the roadway, his stare hardening toward Jess, "we sort of figured we'd race into town and sort of tree the place a little before we settled down to steady drinkin'."

"Then why did you get off your horses?" Jess asked, beginning to come near the end of his rope with these two. It was all right, up to a point, to humor men like these, but beyond that point a man was trading off his self-respect.

Those two faces were suddenly no longer smiling. Jess had touched a sensitive place and all three of them knew it.

They'd *wanted* to tree the town, but something had held them back. It was that something that Jess jostled.

The one nearest the tie rack dropped his right hand straight down. Jess saw, from the corner of his eyes, that trouble had come closer. He kept watching the one out in the dazzling roadway. He decided to try one last time.

"Kind of hot, standin' out here talkin'. Come into the saloon an', like I said, I'll stand the first drinks. We can talk in there."

The crisis had come. Singing Springs lay somnolently in midday sun blast. The sidewalks were empty, a powerful drowsiness was over the land, horses stood here and there with heads hanging. Except for those men in front of Buster Hilton's saloon, probably no one else in town knew that death was there in the roadway's shimmering heat.

Then a new voice spoke up, sounding soft and almost lazy. "Hey, cowboy," this voice said from behind the one near the hitch rack, "I'm going to give you some real sound advice. Take your hand off that gun. And you, out there in the roadway . . . better do a heap more thinking before you brave up enough to make your play."

Jess knew who owned that voice, but he didn't move his eyes one inch to look up where Fawn-Colored-Coat was leaning in the overhang shade. That man by the horses did, though. He turned very slowly, very carefully, until he had the coated, lanky young stranger in his sight.

"And who the hell do you think you are, buttin' in?" he asked.

There was no answer. The stranger up there in the shade was watching the other fired-up buck out in the roadway. He knew, as well as Jess Wright knew, that the one who had spoken had lost all his edginess now, seeing that he and his partner were flanked.

The one out in the roadway was of a different stripe. He heard that voice, placed it, and made his instantaneous decision. And he was fast, faster than anyone Jess Wright had ever seen before. He whipped half around from the middle without moving either foot. He went for that tied-down gun in its greased holster in a blur of speed.

There was a stunning report as a .45 exploded from under the saloon's overhang. Jess, his own gun just clearing leather, had time, for a fraction of a second, to be astonished. He was no slouch with a gun, not after over twenty years of making his living with one, but that gunshot had come while his front sight was still curving over holster leather.

Out in the lemon-yellow roadway that twisted shape flinched. Its head swung forward, and a hat fell forward into roadway dust. That moving, fisted right hand with its blue-black steel blur, ceased moving. The booted feet shuffled back as though to brace themselves, never made it, and the cowboy fell quietly forward on his face, dead as dun-colored dust spurted upward from where he'd landed.

The other one, back by the horses, never completed his draw. He'd started too late. Jess had him covered as he said reedily: "Steady, don't make a move!"

Very gradually the remaining cowboy dropped his pistol back and removed his hand from its black rubber stock, came fully around, and stared disbelievingly out where his partner lay with a flatness, a stillness, that had no counterpart among the living. He seemed not to believe what his own eyes showed him.

Jess went across, took away that holstered six-gun, stepped on out where the dead one lay, toed him over onto his back, gazed into the handsome, wild face, then put up his gun, bent, took the dead one's hat, and placed it over his drying eyes, over his sag-jawed dead face, straightened up, and blew out a long, ragged breath as he gazed up where Fawn-Colored-Coat was still slouching against that overhang upright post, his fisted .45 pointing earthward.

"Right through the heart," Jess said. "Dead center, mister."

Fawn-Colored-Coat nodded, swung, and gazed over at the surviving man. "You take advice better'n your friend," he said very gently. "Now you'd better toss him across his saddle and head on out." He put up his gun, straightened away from the post, and gazed back out to where the dead man lay. "Unless, of course, you want to take it up where your pardner left it."

The other man didn't want that. He went out, lifted his friend, lugged him over to the tie rack, and settled him face down across his saddle. Jess helped him lash the body down. Jess also held the horse while the other one got astride his own animal.

He said: "We got a boothill cemetery here in Singing Springs. It's better'n some hole out in the desert where the coyotes'll dig up your friend. You're welcome to a plot if you want it."

The cowboy looked briefly at Jess, his face white to the hairline, then reached for the reins of the dead man's animal at the same time as he stared straight at Fawn-Colored-Coat. "You just made the biggest . . . and last . . . mistake of your life, mister," he said very softly. "By this time tomorrow you'll be as dead as *he* is. Let go the horse, Sheriff. . . ."

Jess stood back, watching the live one lead the dead one back across the boiling roadway out of Singing Springs the way they had both entered it not more than twenty minutes earlier. There were a lot of other spectators, too, who saw this grisly exodus. They had been drawn to the roadway by that sudden, loud gunshot.

Chapter Three

The man in the coat said: "Sheriff, you should've asked him who they were."

Jess came right back with a question of his own. "I got a better idea. I'll ask you who you are."

Fawn-Colored-Coat put a hand upon the upright post and gazed thoughtfully out at Jess Wright. He didn't say what his name was. He said: "Sheriff, you'd never have made it. How's it feel to be alive when you shouldn't be?"

Jess turned that one over and over. It was true enough. He couldn't have beaten the dead one to the draw, and, boxed in like that between them, even if he could have, the other one would have gotten him. "All right," he said, strolling on over. "I'm obliged to you. Now, about your name . . . ?"

The tawny-eyed, loose, and easy stranger mirthlessly smiled. "Hell, Sheriff, I'm a stranger to Singin' Springs and you haven't offered me that free drink yet."

Jess got to feeling a little uncomfortable, not so much at the way he was being toyed with by Fawn-Colored-Coat, but because there were a dozen curious townsmen and cattlemen edging up to hear what was being said. He jerked his head sideward. "Inside," he said a little gruffly. "First drink's on me."

Buster Hilton was behind his bar. Ordinarily Buster didn't wait on customers. He had two bartenders, one for days and one for nights, but this was different; it was, in a way, a special occasion. Buster hadn't had a man killed either inside his saloon or outside it in the roadway in some time. He was as

58

curious about the lanky stranger as everyone else was, so he put his dark gaze forward and waited.

As Jess settled sideways against Buster's bar, the stranger with him lifted his eyes to say: "Couple of whiskies."

Buster nodded, and moved off.

"The name is Shad Adams, Sheriff, an' now you know as much as you knew before," said the stranger, "because I'm not listed on any of your Wanted posters."

Wright filed away that name. Shad would be for Shadrach Adams. Well, Adams could be his name, or just a name he'd settled upon. He couldn't recall having heard the name before.

"You're good with a gun," said Jess.

Hilton brought the whisky, set the bottle and glasses before the two of them, drew forth a wiping rag from his belt, and began swiping at the clean bar top with it. Shad Adams didn't touch his drink. He leaned there, watching Hilton and looked mildly amused. Finally he turned his back upon Buster and said loudly enough for Hilton to hear: "You've got quite a little town here, Sheriff. Everyone wants to be in on things . . . *after* they happen." Then Shad lifted his glass and tossed off the whisky.

The implication had been quite clear. Buster straightened up with an indignant look on his face, turned, and walked farther down his bar where other men were signaling for service. But he remembered that innuendo because he was no coward and resented being obliquely accused of being one.

"It happened too fast for folks to know," said Jess. "Anyway, it was my job, not the town's."

"Yeah? And if I hadn't been around to bail you out, they'd have had a dead lawman. Then what, Sheriff?"

There was more than just Shad Adams's confidence to annoy Jess. There was also the stranger's ability to put his finger squarely on a fact as he bluntly spoke of it.

"You're young," said Jess, reaching for his glass. "You've got a lot to learn." He threw back his head, swallowed once, and made a face. That whisky had been as green as grass.

Adams half twisted to gaze around. The Cinch-Up was full now. Men lined the bar, sat at the tables, or stood about in little cliques, sometimes looking his way, sometimes quietly talking. He looked back. "Ought to get ten percent for bringin' in this business, Sheriff. Tell me . . . is that dark-lookin' feller the owner of this place?"

"He is. His name's Buster Hilton."

Shad lowered his face and concentrated upon turning his empty glass in its little sticky puddle atop the bar. "Yeah, I've heard of Buster Hilton. Used to be quite a boy in his day."

Jess was thinking of something else. He said: "Adams, I don't know who those two were, but the one still alive looked like he meant what he said out there . . . about you. Unless you've got business here in Singin' Springs, I reckon you'd better get your horse and head out."

"Why, you figure I can't handle that one, too?"

"No. Because I don't want the town shot up."

"Oh."

Shad turned. He was a handsome man with large blue eyes and even features. He seemed to have a habit of half smiling, almost as though, while his lips and his eyes were indulgently amiable, his mind was being coldly practical. The smile, Jess thought, was a sort of shield, a deception. Taken all in all, this young gunman—and Jess had no doubt at all but that was what Shad Adams was—was about as easy to figure out, to typecast and catalogue, as the man in the moon.

The batwing doors shivered open, swung closed behind a newcomer, and Jess automatically looked over. This was the tough-faced, gray, and grizzled older man who'd gotten off the stage not too long before, and, although this man wore a suit of clothes and a small, stiff-brimmed hat, plus a necktie, he definitely was not a city man. Aside from the gun bulge under his coat on the right side, he had the perpetually slitted, bright, hard eyes, the sun-blasted features, and the thin-lipped mouth of a range man. Probably a cattleman passing through, Jess thought, or a stock buyer.

This stranger hiked on over to the bar, rapped for a drink, and didn't look right or left until Buster took him his shot of rotgut. Then he downed this, half turned, and ran a slow, blank stare at Shad Adams. Jess noticed that look; he also noticed how Shad returned it, as though he didn't really know who that older man was, but also as though he had some idea why he was here.

In a quiet voice Jess said: "Know him?"

In the same soft tone that didn't carry any farther than where they stood Shad drawled: "Nope. But I can tell you one thing, Sheriff . . . that one's a Texan." Shad lowered his head and went on toying with the empty glass. "Tell you somethin' else, too, Sheriff. He's not here because he likes the desert."

"Cow buyer," mused Jess.

Shad turned his head. He was wearing that smile again, only now it was genuine. "Walk down there an' look under his coat. He's got a gun on the right side an' a badge on his vest on the left side."

Jess didn't move. He gazed from Shad to the stranger and back again. "You said you didn't know him."

"I don't, but I caught the scent when he stepped through those doors yonder." Shad straightened up and turned away. "Thanks for the drink," he murmured. "See you again, Sheriff." He crossed the room with almost every eye upon him, passed out of sight through the batwing doors, and finally the talk around the room came out in the open with its questions and its speculative answers.

Buster Hilton padded down to where Jess was leaning, picked up the coin Wright had put down, hooked both elbows over the bar, and looked toward the door where Adams had disappeared. "They're sayin' he's the fastest man with a gun that ever hit town, Jess. How about that? You was out there . . . you seen him . . . how about it?"

"True, Buster, true," assented the sheriff succinctly. "Never saw the beat of that draw of his."

"He's pretty young, Jess. Not more'n twenty-one or -two."

"I know that."

"Well, he's been practicin' since he was a button, then. They don't get that fast over-night, you know."

Jess looked down his nose at swarthy, beetle-browed Buster Hilton. This conversation was beginning to ruffle him a little. "So he's been at it a long time," he murmured.

Buster looked up quickly. "Saved your bacon, didn't he?"

"That's what he told me, Buster."

Hilton rubbed his square, massive jaw and rocked his head over to one side. "Cocky an' a mite smart-alecky. Kind of hard, right off the bat, to know just what to make of his kind, isn't it?"

"I'll tell you this much, Buster . . . don't push him into a gunfight."

Hilton stopped stroking his jaw, looked up sardonically, and drew back off his bar. "I didn't quite have that in mind," he said. "Anyway, I got a notion that whatever brought him here to Singin' Springs is more likely to be in your department than mine."

As Buster turned to walk off, that narrow-eyed, grizzled stranger strolled over and leaned on the bar beside Jess Wright. "Barman," he said, "fetch two more drinks, will you?

One for the sheriff an' one for me." This man then turned, pushed out a thick paw toward Jess, and introduced himself. "Fred Huff, Sheriff. Texas Ranger."

Jess shook, released the other man's hand, and stared as Huff lifted his coat to disclose, on the left side of his vest, the small German steel circlet that was his badge.

"Watched you and that young feller talkin'," Huff said, studying Jess closely, "and sort of got the impression he didn't hit you just right." As he dropped his coat back into place and turned to reach for the drink Buster had brought up, he said: "Funny thing about his kind, Sheriff . . . even though they're almost always within the law, they leave a bad taste in a man's mouth."

Jess watched the Ranger without making a move to pick up the drink at his elbow. "His kind, Mister Huff . . . just what *is* his kind?"

Huff drank, set the glass aside, and looked around. "Bounty hunter, Sheriff. That there young buck's Shadrach Adams."

Huff leaned there, eyeing Jess and waiting. Wright understood that the name should mean something to him, knew that Huff was expecting him to register surprise or apprehension, or something like that, but try as he might he simply could not recall ever having heard the name Shadrach Adams before.

Jess shrugged. "Sorry, Mister Huff . . . don't know him."

Huff pursed his lips, looked around the room, out over the tops of the batwing doors out where midday heat blast lay in fiercely shimmering waves of gelatin-like painful light, and said to Jess without looking at him: "Well, Sheriff, Singing Springs is a long way from Tucumcari. I noticed, too, as I looked your town over, there's no telegraph line." Huff swung back to put his habitually slitted eyes upon Wright.

"So maybe it's understandable that you've never heard of me, of Shad Adams, or of the Wiltons."

"Wiltons? You mean the Wilton gang? Sure I've heard of them, Mister Huff. We get the newspapers when the stage fetches 'em along." Jess was beginning to have a bad feeling. He leaned down a little toward the shorter but thicker man. "Are you telling me the Wiltons are around Singing Springs, Ranger?"

"Right here in your town, Sheriff," said Fred Huff softly, so softly no one but Jess Wright heard him say it. "One of them, the youngest, died right here in the center of your roadway this morning."

Jess stood like a statue for the moment it took for him to absorb this. "You mean that young curly wolf Adams shot?"

"The same, Sheriff. Johnny Wilton, the youngest of the Wilton brothers. Care for another drink? Oh, excuse me. You haven't finished yours yet."

"And you," said Jess, brushing past that reference to the drink, "you're not just passing through either, are you?"

"Nope. I've been trailing the Wiltons since they broke into the bank up at Tucumcari and afterward shot their way out of town. They left three dead men up there. But before that . . . well . . . it's a long story. Texas has a five thousand dollar reward on the heads of Stub Wilton, Frank Wilton, and Lance Wilton. On young Johnny there's only one thousand. He only joined his brothers this spring. He was at the Tucumcari robbery, but it's a mite early for rewards to be posted on him for that yet."

"Which one was that feller with Johnny Wilton this morning?"

"None of the Wilton boys, Sheriff, but they always have three, four more renegades riding with them. It's quite a gang. Memberships change pretty often." Ranger Fred Huff made a wry face. "Mortality rate's pretty high amongst 'em. I never saw that one before. I'd guess he's some local cowboy or punk gunfighter they picked up in one of the towns they passed through on their way south toward the Mexican line. That's where they usually head for, after a big haul."

Jess turned very slowly, picked up the drink, downed it, and leaned over the bar. The Wilton gang of outlaws was notorious, had been notorious for ten years, and, while they were almost legendary because they hadn't ever been apprehended and the rewards had been piling up on them, most small town lawmen like Jess Wright just sort of lived with the knowledge that these men were loose and likely to strike anywhere at any time, but never really considered it plausible that they themselves would run across the gang because the Wiltons were after the big money that was only found in the big towns.

But this was different. Clearly, in their race for the border, the Wiltons had known where Singing Springs was, but just as clearly they wouldn't bother with a town so small and insignificant, either. Ordinarily, anyway. But this was different. One of the Wiltons had been shot to death in Singing Springs.

Jess eased around toward Fred Huff. He studied the grizzled, weathered Texas Ranger for a moment of long silence. First Shad Adams, then this Texas lawman. "Funny thing," he murmured. "I smelt trouble in the air, Ranger. Felt it in my guts, when I rolled out of bed this morning. But you know what trouble is in a place like Singing Springs?"

"I know, Sheriff. I've been at this law enforcement business longer'n you have. I'm past fifty years old." Huff gently nodded as he met Jess's gaze. "Trouble in a place like Singing Springs is a drunk cowboy shootin' out windows, or it's a pair of freighters brawling out in the roadway over some Mex girl, or it's a two-bit horse thief caught in the act by a cowman. Am I right?"

"Right as rain."

"Well, when I got off the stage today, Sheriff, I had a funny little thought about your town. I thought that maybe this is it . . . maybe this is the end of a ten-year trail. Now I've been in a lot of towns since I've been after the Wiltons . . . hell . . . I can't even begin to recollect all their names from Texas into New Mexico Territory . . . but I had this odd little hunch. Then, when I looked through my rooming house window and saw who that was out there in the roadway goin' for his gun . . . young Johnny Wilton . . . and saw him get killed out there . . . Sheriff, I *knew* this was the town I'd been riding toward for a long, long time."

"But this bounty hunter, this Shad Adams . . . is he tryin' to get the Wiltons all by himself?"

Huff nodded his head. "Yeah. But maybe I wasn't exactly fair about Shad. I don't like him. Still an' all, a man ought to give another man his due. Shad's brother was a Texas Ranger. The Wiltons killed him at Eagle Pass in Texas two years back. We offered Shad his brother's badge. He turned it down. He said he wanted the Wiltons, but he didn't want any damned badge to hinder him in the way he got them. Well, today he got one, Sheriff, so today your town stepped smack dab into the middle of a genuine blood feud. And Sheriff . . . don't think for a minute the Wiltons will overlook young Johnny's killing."

Chapter Four

It was nearly five in the evening before Jess saw Shadrach Adams again. He was over in front of the livery barn talking to Angie Miflin, and in the adjoining building Brigham Pruett was idling in his doorway, smoking a cigar. Jess had told dark-complexioned Buster Hilton what Ranger Huff had said, and Buster, after a long moment of total silence while he poured himself a double shot, downed it, and afterward thunderously coughed, had said that he'd known the Wiltons once, years back when they were just getting started.

"Bad, Jess, bad as they come, all of 'em. Mean clean through. They'd as soon set fire to this town in the night and pot-shoot folks by the firelight, as belly up to a bar and drink whisky. Of all the lousy damned luck . . . why did it have to be Singing Springs? Hell's bells, I came here because we're so far from everything. There are others here who came for the same reason, too. Now look what we got . . . all because of that damned Shad Adams."

Jess was thinking of this conversation now as he loitered across the way, waiting for Angie to stroll off so he could walk on over and brace Shad Adams. He knew exactly what he was going to tell him: *Get on your horse and get to hell out of this town.*

And he *did* tell him that some fifteen minutes later after Angie had gone on and he caught the easy-moving younger man down in front of the saddle shop. Shad smiled his easy smile while looking straight into Jess's eyes. "Afraid I can't do that, Sheriff. You see, I've got a reason for being in Singing

Springs, and I can't leave until. . . ."

"I know all about your reason . . . the Wilton gang," growled Jess. "Well, you're entitled to one thousand dollar's reward for killing the youngest of them, and I'll sign an affidavit as sheriff of Yaqui County that I witnessed that killing. But that's the end of it, Shad. You fork your horse and get out of my town."

"Sheriff," said Shad, his smile becoming slightly strained. "Johnny Wilton died facing you . . . not me. Sure, I shot him, but d'you think for a minute that's going to stop Frank and Stub and Lance from coming here looking for you? No, sir, not on your tintype it isn't. So . . . I'll sort of hang around to back your play when they ride in. Excuse me now, I got to go pay the blacksmith for fittin' my horse up with new shoes all around."

Shad Adams stepped around Jess and walked southward. Jess turned to look after him, but he didn't sing out. In fact, the next person to speak was Brigham Pruett from his saddle shop doorway.

"Step inside, Sheriff," the saddle maker invited, tossing away his stub of a cigar, and afterward, when they were quite alone in the coolness of the shop, Pruett ran a thick set of fingers through his heavy mane and said wryly: "He's right, Jess. He's as fast with a gun as any man I ever saw. You need him maybe even more than he needs you. And that talk about the Wiltons . . . that was right, too. They'll be coming to Singing Springs. Maybe if it'd been Stub or Lance or even Frank, and they were pressed close, they might have let it slide for a few months, but that was young Johnny. They won't let ten dozen posses stop 'em from avenging him. He was the baby of the family."

Jess leaned upon Pruett's counter, thumbed back his hat, and mildly swore. Outside in the roadway the usual traffic was passing back and forth, slouched riders in from the ranches, battered wagons with screeching, greaseless axles, strollers and shoppers moving across his line of vision. He scarcely saw them.

Pruett went around behind the counter and resumed work at a saddle he was making. A solitary blue-tailed fly buzzed tirelessly in wide circles. Jess turned, watched Pruett's powerful, scarred big hands smooth out damp leather, and it came to him very gradually that Brigham Pruett had spoken of the Wiltons as a man who hadn't just heard of them. He'd said, for instance, with a voice full of grave conviction that the others wouldn't overlook the killing of young Johnny.

Jess regarded Pruett's heavy-featured face and big, sloping shoulders with fresh interest. He groped around for some way of starting a fresh conversation, for some way of getting it out of Pruett just how much he really knew of the Wiltons. But Pete Odell walked in out of the sun blast, mopped his neck, and blew out a big ragged breath, saying: "Damn but she's a hot one today." That shattered whatever mood of privacy had theretofore existed in the shop.

Pruett looked up and nodded, but he didn't speak. He seemed to Jess to be deep in some private thoughts of his own.

Odell crossed to the counter, leaned there, and watched Pruett work for a while. He looked casually around at Jess, his eyes speculative. "You know who that young buck was who got shot in the road this morning?"

"Yes," said Jess. "I know. Who told you . . . Buster?"

"Yeah, but it's all over town. Charley Miflin also told me. So did Sam Potts over at the livery barn." Odell paused to glance back at Brigham Pruett. The saddle maker was obviously listening, but he neither looked up nor spoke. "I reckon we've got a real mess on our hands now," said Odell, sounding less worried than interested.

Now Pruett looked up. "Trouble, yes," he said quietly. "But it might not be as bad as it looks."

Jess and Pete Odell gazed at the saddle maker. Pruett lifted his thick shoulders and dropped them. "There was those two game-cocks that rode in today, part of the Wilton gang. Then there was that other one . . . Shadrach Adams who killed young Wilton. But there was another stranger hit Singing Springs today . . . saw him get off the stage through my front window. His name's Fred Huff."

Jess's eyes widened slightly. He hadn't mentioned Huff, and he was confident no one besides himself knew Huff's name or who he was, let alone why he was in Singing Springs.

"Fred Huff," went on Brigham Pruett, "is one of the toughest old razorbacks that ever came down the line. He's about the only Texas Ranger that, when folks mention his name in the Indian Territory, half the boys get up out of their chairs and walk out, get on their horses, and ride."

Pete Odell was watching Pruett, too, now, and after a slightly awkward silence, when the saddle maker stopped speaking, Odell said: "Brigham, for an itinerant saddle an' harness man, you seem to know a heap of folks."

That was exactly what Jess Wright was also thinking, but he wouldn't have said it straight out like that. Jess wasn't as blunt and direct as Pete was.

Pruett returned their gazes without blinking. He shrugged finally, put his hands upon the drying seating leather in front of him, and dropped his head as he mumbled: "No mystery to that. I built saddles and mended harness in the Indian Territory for a while. Been in Texas, too. You can't make anything out of that, Odell."

Pete said quickly: "Wasn't tryin' to, Brigham. Anyway, if this Huff's all you say, why, then, I expect we're even better off than I figured we might be." Odell turned to Wright.

"Jess, how long do you figure it'll take the Wiltons to get here?"

Jess had thought about this some time before, so he had no difficulty in answering. "Depends on just whereabouts they are. If they're heading south fast, as Ranger Huff said, because they shot up some men in Tucumcari, it might be several days. But if they're somewhere east or west of town, about parallel to us, why I'd say maybe tomorrow, Pete."

"Get up a posse," exclaimed the rooming house owner. "Organize the cow outfits, make a big sashay out an' around, Jess. How many men they supposed to have with 'em?"

"Who knows? Maybe eight, ten . . . or twenty."

"Didn't this Huff feller know?"

"No one knows for sure, Pete."

Pruett said solemnly: "That's right, Odell. And for what it's worth, I'll give you a word of advice, Sheriff . . . don't do what Odell's suggestin', don't get up a little army an' go hunting them, because they'll see you miles before you see them, and they'll get around behind you, hit this town, and burn it to the ground. I know."

"How do you know?" demanded Pete Odell, but Jess Wright broke in here before Pruett had time to answer, saying for Pete to go on back to his rooming house, hunt up Fred Huff, and tell Huff that Jess wanted to see him down at the jailhouse.

Odell left, and Jess watched him walk across the shimmering roadway with his back to Pruett as he drawled: "Brigham, I'm not a man who was raised believing one man's got the right to ask another man personal questions. But if the day comes when you want to tell me anything, I'll be around."

Jess straightened up off the counter, still without looking back, and strolled on out of the shop, turned right, and went along through fierce heat to his jailhouse office. Pruett hadn't said a single thing back there at the saddle shop that had been founded upon speculation. After twenty years of learning how to read men, Jess Wright was as sure of that now as he'd ever been sure of anything. Somewhere, somehow, Brigham Pruett had known the Wiltons.

Jess had just hung up his hat when Fred Huff came across from the direction of the rooming house. He was no longer wearing his store-bought clothes, but was now attired in the loose-fitting faded shirt and trousers of a range man. He wasn't wearing his Ranger badge, Jess noticed, but then he wouldn't have been anyway, because a Ranger's badge carried no weight outside Texas. But one thing Jess *did* notice was that Fred Huff wore his .45 low and lashed down.

The moment he stepped through the door, Huff screwed up his face and said: "Sheriff, that feller Odell who runs the rooming house seems to hear a lot. He was telling me about some of the local businessmen around Singing Springs."

"I can imagine," muttered Jess, motioning toward a chair. "But I wouldn't put too much stock in gossip, Mister Huff."

"Gossip? When I saw that dark feller up at the saloon, Sheriff, I recognized him right off the bat. That's. . . ."

"Buster Hilton. Sure, he's been here quite a spell, and he's one of our best men, Ranger."

Huff looked around at the chair Jess had indicated. He eyed it as though it might be a sleeping snake, but he eased down upon it.

Jess riffled through a stack of Wanted posters covered with dust, selected several, and spread them out. He was gazing at the hard, ruthless faces of the Wilton brothers. There wasn't much similarity among those faces: between Stub and Lance there was a recognizable affinity, but Frank Wilton looked altogether different. Even his description was different.

Where neither Lance nor Stub was very tall, Frank Wilton was an even six feet. Even their hair was different. Lance and Stub had Indian-like straight black hair. Frank's hair was lighter and curly.

Huff, seeing how Jess was studying those pictures, said dryly: "I wouldn't try to memorize 'em, Sheriff, because you're going to get to meet them directly or I sure miss my guess."

The stage came rattling in, filling Jess's little office with noise. He stepped to the door to watch passengers alight. Right behind him came Ranger Huff. Two men got off. They both looked around at the town, then caught their carpet-bags, tossed down by the shotgun guard, and struck out for Odell's place.

"Never saw either of them before," said Huff. "Did you?"

Jess shook his head. "Peddlers more'n likely. This time of year they come an' go." He turned back into the office, dropped down at his desk, and gazed over at the Texan. "Odd how things work out sometimes. Here I am, sittin' in the middle of nowhere out in the New Mexico desert. The town's quiet, the countryside's quiet, and the most I'd expect anyway would be maybe some Mex horse thieves or cattle rustlers sneakin' over the line in the night . . . or maybe a drunk cowboy or two . . . and here, in a twinklin' . . . I'm in the middle of a feud, a killin', a nest of bank robbers with the Texas Rangers on their trail, and the Lord only knows what other troubles."

"It could be worse," said Huff grimly. "The whole gang could have decided to ride into your town for a little fun on the way south. Then you know what you'd have, Sheriff? I'll tell you . . . you more'n likely would be so dead you wouldn't even know or care. That's how it *could've* been. It's happened like that in other towns no larger than Singing Springs. If you ask me, Sheriff Wright, you're lucky. Damned lucky. You can dislike Shad Adams as much as I do, but don't sell the boy short. In a showdown I wouldn't ask for any other man beside me. You're lucky, Sheriff. Don't you ever think otherwise."

Chapter Five

If he was lucky, Jess thought, then luck was pretty much a relative thing. If he was lucky *now*, under these circumstances, he wondered just how he could be much worse off by being *un*lucky.

"Well," he philosophized to Fred Huff, "one time in a saloon over in Abilene I heard an old man say that every day a feller lives past thirty is a bonus. I've lived almost six years past thirty."

Huff smiled. "Quite a bunch of bonuses," he said. "Me, I've lost count."

"And the Wiltons?" Jess asked quietly. "Usually their kind doesn't last so long, Ranger. Take the ones a feller's heard of . . . Jesse James, Bill Hickok, William Bonney, Clay Allison . . . all pretty young when they cashed in. What's made the Wiltons different?"

"I'll tell you, Sheriff. Their ma."

Jess looked surprised.

Huff solemnly inclined his grizzled head. "Yes, sir, their mother. Her name was Alicia . . . now that's a real high-toned name, but Alicia Wilton was born just plain Alice Flannery. She married Lance Wilton when she was sixteen an' he was thirty . . . and fresh out of prison for murder and train robbery. Old Lance got killed seven years ago blowing a safe over at Stillwater in the Nations. Alice changed her name to Alicia, and she set to work makin' her two boys the terror of the Nations."

"Two boys, Ranger?"

"I'm comin' to that, Sheriff. She married another feller the year after Lance got killed. He had a half-grown boy she took under her wing. That was Frank. His name's not really Wilton. She turned that kid into one of the cruelest, deadliest buckaroos alive. By the time his pa packed up and left old Alice, his own boy had turned against him. That one's Frank Wilton . . . he took the name Wilton, too. Now young Johnny, the one who died here in the roadway, he was old Alicia's pride an' joy. Frank and Stub and Lance doted on him, too. Now do you get the picture, Sheriff?"

"I get it."

A lean shadow darkened the office doorway. Shad Adams walked in, gazed straight at Huff and nodded, turned sideways and said: "Sheriff, I'm going for a little ride out of town. Figured I'd tell you first, just in case I don't get back. I'll look off to the west first, then over to the east."

Jess thoughtfully gazed over at Adams. "And suppose what you're lookin' for is southward . . . what then?"

"I'll find what I'm looking for."

"A bullet in the back," said the Ranger, rising from his chair. "Adams, you don't remember me, but I'm Fred Huff. I rode with your brother the last two years of his life."

Shad studied Huff over a long interval of full silence before saying softly: "Sure, I had a hunch I'd seen you somewhere before, at the saloon. Reckon I should say I'm glad to see you, Ranger . . . only I'm not."

Huff's eyes puckered ironically. "Don't worry, I won't get in your way, not when you do stupid things like ridin' out alone to hunt 'em up. You're forgettin' those boys know more about watching back trails and signalin' with belt buckles an' stalkin' men on foot than the damned Indians know. And you're also forgettin' the most important thing of all . . . they won't be running now. They'll be headin' straight for this town. Go ahead and ride out, Shad. They'll gut-shoot you just like they did your brother . . . without givin' you a chance even to draw."

Jess, watching the faces of those two, saw Shad turn pale and saw Huff turn hard. They stared straight at one another for a long time before Shad looked around at Jess again as he reached into a shirt pocket and extracted a folded paper.

"Read it," he said, tossing the paper onto Wright's desk. "Then add your affidavit to it so I can collect that lousy one thousand dollars for Johnny Wilton. I'll pick it up on my way back through town, and mail it." He started to turn about in the doorway to depart, paused a moment, and said to Ranger Huff: "Nothin' worse than a bounty hunter, is there, Ranger, unless it's one that doesn't care how he kills his prey?" Then Shad Adams disappeared up the plank walk in the direction of Sam Potts's livery barn.

Huff sighed audibly, and reseated himself. It was hot in the thick-walled little office. The air wasn't stirring at all. He mopped sweat off his face and neck with a blue bandanna, shoved the thing into a hip pocket, and gazed over where Jess was reading the letter Shad had left behind.

"If he sat up nights figurin' ways to make folks dislike him, he couldn't be any more successful at it," Huff said. "And yet, you know, they tell me before his brother was killed, Shad was a happy-go-lucky cowhand with a big smile for everyone."

Jess offered the letter to Huff, but the Ranger waved it away. He made a face. Jess put the letter aside, got up, and strolled over to lean in the doorway where a faint breath of hot air was usually stirring.

Outside, Singing Springs was quiet. The east side of the roadway was a burnished red from the lowering late-day sun. In front of Odell's rooming house an old man was indifferently sweeping the sidewalk, and up at Buster Hilton's saloon two cowboys stood impatiently just outside the swinging doors waiting for a third ranch hand to finish with his horse at the tie rack.

"Tell me something," he said casually to Fred Huff without looking around. "Is it likely the Wiltons will have any idea who shot Johnny?"

Huff was yawning. He finished that before pushing up out of his chair and stepping over also to feel that little tantalizing rush of roiled air. "Depends on how well that lad who was with Johnny can describe Adams."

"They know he's after them?"

"Yeah, they know that. He almost got Stub over in Bartlesville one night in a saloon. Another time he. . . ."

"Whoa," broke in Jess softly, straightening up. "Look yonder."

Huff edged closer and peered out into the sooty early evening. Across the way and a few doors northward, in front of Pete Odell's building, those two men who'd come in on the noon stage were lounging in gloomy shade staring straight over at the livery barn where Shad Adams was standing out front talking to Sam Potts, a short, paunchy individual with a shiny scalp and sly hound-dog eyes. As the pair of peace officers watched, one of those strangers said something sharp to his companion, and that second stranger abruptly turned and faded inside the rooming house.

Up the road Shad passed over some money to Sam Potts, toed in, and sprang up over leather. He was turning his horse when that stranger reëmerged from Odell's place. He had two booted Winchester carbines in his hands, one of which he passed over to his partner, then the pair of them stepped out, moving down into the roadway on an angling course bound for the livery barn.

"Well, well," said Fred Huff quietly. "I reckon the Wiltons aren't too far away, after all. Sent those two on ahead probably because they wouldn't be known hereabouts. Sent 'em in on the stage, too, just like they were peddlers or travelers. I tell you, Sheriff, they're smart. It's Frank. He's the brains of the gang."

Jess stepped out onto the plank walk, saying: "Come on. I thought maybe Adams would at least get a few miles out."

As they paced up toward Sam Potts's barn, Huff said: "I reckon this answers a question you asked, Sheriff. I reckon that other one who visited Singing Springs described Johnny's killer plain enough."

Jess had nothing more to say until, within sighting distance of the livery barn's long, wetted-down earth alleyway, he saw Sam and the two strangers talking together while Sam's hostler rigged out two horses.

At his side as they entered the barn, the Texas Ranger breathed a little warning. "Careful, Sheriff. Be damned careful. They'll have other weapons besides the carbines."

But Jess and Fred Huff had an advantage. The backs of both those strangers were to them, and, although Sam Potts saw Jess and his companion walking up, Sam went on talking. He was used to Sheriff Wright's strolling in any time of the night or day to gossip a little.

They were very close, less than six feet off, when the hostler looked around and, broadly smiling, said: "Howdy, Sheriff. Be with you in a minute."

The two strangers stiffened. Jess saw that even in the building's murky evening gloom. He dropped his right hand straight down and said: "Steady, boys. Don't turn around and keep your hands right where they are."

Sam Potts's mouth dropped open; his eyes slowly bulged wide. Off to one side, where he'd stepped, Huff drew and cocked his .45. It was that little lethal sound that froze even the hostler, who was a good fifty feet away.

"Drop the carbines," Jess ordered.

The two strangers, still with their backs to the law, obeyed. Jess shot Huff a glance. The Ranger nodded. Jess stepped in close, plucked away the belt guns of their prisoners, told them to place their hands behind their heads and to turn around. The outlaws obeyed, but slowly, and one of them, a man with a knife scar up into his hairline to the right of his temple, also spoke as he turned.

"Just what the hell do you think you're doing, Sheriff? We came in here to hire a couple of horses and have a look around the countryside. We're travelin' men. What're you tryin' to make out of that? What law have we broken?"

"None," said Jess. "But that's only because you didn't get the chance. Sam, back away from those two."

Potts backed away. His hostler still stood like a statue fifty feet on down the runway, looking flabbergasted. The man who hadn't spoken was staring straight at Jess Wright with murderous anger unmistakably in his eyes.

"We're going to take a walk down to the jailhouse," said Jess, "so, when you walk out of here, turn right. There'll be two guns behind you, boys. If you're tired of livin', make a break for it. Now start walkin'."

Both the men were dark from days under a blazing sun. Both of them had the unkempt, tawny look of men long away from civilization. Their hair was too long and their clothing was shiny from wear, and yet an obvious effort had been made to erase the most obvious indications of this. Now, as they walked between Huff and Jess Wright, the knife-scarred one looked bitterly at Jess and said from the corner of his thin-lipped mouth: "Sheriff, you're a fool. All this'll get you is a bellyful of lead, one of these days."

Huff stepped up as Jess started along behind his prisoners. He said softly: "I could wish we'd captured younger, less experienced ones. These two won't talk. I know their kind."

Huff was correct. After Jess barred his office door and stood back while the Ranger frisked his prisoners, turning up two boot knives and two hide-out little belly-guns of large caliber, Jess put up his six-gun and asked the men their names. They sneered at him. He asked where the Wiltons were, and they asked who the Wiltons were. He then asked them why, if they weren't part of the Wilton gang, they'd tried to ride out after Shad Adams, and to this the knife-scarred renegade gave a straight answer.

"When're you goin' to get tired of askin' questions, Sheriff? If the Wiltons want your town, they'll take it. As for that feller who rode out a while back . . . he's a murderer, Sheriff, and murderers got a way of havin' accidents when they're out a few miles from a town. Anythin' wrong with that?"

"Sure, there's something wrong with it, mister. Shootin' a man in the back makes *two* murderers, and the law doesn't like the odds to pile up like that."

Scar-Face made a flinty smile while his partner sulked. He said: "Two or ten, what's the difference? Sheriff, you're in a bad spot. You want to be around the house next Christmas? Get on your horse and take a trip. Go up north on business or something. Stay away from Singin' Springs for the next five days. It'd be a shame if you weren't around next Christmas to fill the socks for the kids, wouldn't it?"

"Sure would," said Jess Wright laconically. "Especially since I live at the rooming house, don't have any kids, and don't even have a wife. When are they coming?"

"Who, Sheriff, you talkin' about?"

Jess sighed, and put his head to one side for the length of

time it took him to appraise that evilly grinning outlaw. "You know," he said conversationally, "I've often wondered if maybe I couldn't take on two like you boys at the same time and make mincemeat out of you."

Fred Huff eased down upon the edge of the office desk and looked pleased about something. "You know, that's one thing about small-town law I always approved of. Now, down where I come from, we got justices of the peace and lawyers and circuit judges thicker'n hair on a dog's back, so we dassn't knock out any teeth or bust any noses. But in those little out of the way places like Singing Springs, it's different. It's more like the law used to be twenty, thirty years back." Huff got up off the desk edge, smiling. "I'll hold your gun, Sheriff."

Scar-Face and his partner straightened up. They were no longer either sneering or sulking. Each of them took the measure of raw-boned, lanky Jess Wright. Neither of them came within three or four inches of Jess's six feet, two inches, although both were compact, solidly put together men, and tough. It was written all over them that they could, and would, fight.

Jess waited a long moment before he took down a ring of keys and slouched past to open his cell-room door and jerk his head at the prisoners. "Think it over," he told those two. "You've got all night to do it. Give us some answers by morning, or I'm going to see if maybe I can't bloody you boys up a little. Get in there!"

Fred Huff was leaning in the doorway when Jess returned from locking up his prisoners. As he hung the key ring back upon its wall peg, Huff said: "Shad's slipping, Sheriff. To my knowledge that's the first time he ever failed to look back. Must be something else on his mind."

Jess thought instantly of pretty little Angie Miflin. "There is," he grunted. "Come on, let's go get some supper over at the Mexican's place. One thing's sure . . . the Wiltons won't hit Singing Springs tonight."

After locking the outside office door, they stepped forth into the growing evening.

Chapter Six

It was early the following morning, after news of what had transpired at Sam Potts's barn had spread all over town, that Charley Miflin came to see Jess at the jailhouse. Charley was a powerfully built man, tough and round and durable. He'd come to Singing Springs from the opposite direction most of the other settlers had come. Charley had come up out of Mexico with little Angie, when she'd been no more than six or seven years of age. Charley was a widower. Folks knew that much about him. He was also an excellent blacksmith, not just at sweating steel tires onto wagon and buggy wheels or at shoeing horses, but also at making handsome iron grilles and delicate filigree work. How he'd come to be down in Mexico or what had later brought him north over the line no one knew and, after so many years, no one cared.

Charley was a hard worker, a sober, quiet man who lived for his lovely daughter and his smithy. In all the years Jess Wright had known him, Charley had never spoken of himself or his past, except once, and that was the night he and Jess had sat in stony agony waiting for the doctor to get to Charley's house from New Castle, a town forty miles east of Singing Springs. That was the night Angie's appendix had been removed, and she'd been drawn back from the edge of the grave.

That was also the night stocky Charley Miflin had told Jess that of all the things he'd done in his lifetime of which he was now deeply ashamed, if the Lord would only spare little Angie he'd dedicate the rest of his life to making up for those things. That was all he'd said, but it was enough. Jess knew then that Charley Miflin had some grisly, dark secrets, otherwise he'd never have spoken quite so intently, so fervently, of the shameful things he'd done.

Now, as Jess was putting on his hat to cross over to the Mexican's place for two trays of food for his prisoners, Charley appeared in the doorway, looking troubled, anxious, and bewildered. "Jess," he said, without even bidding Wright a good morning, "what exactly is behind all the rumors flyin' around town about these Wiltons?"

Jess said blandly: "You've heard as much as I have, Charley. That was the youngest Wilton that died in our roadway. The others aren't far off on their way into Mexico after a raid on Tucumcari. They'll be coming to Singing Springs for revenge. That's about the size of it."

"No," stated the worried blacksmith. "There's more to it than that. Angie's involved."

Jess thought he understood. He said gently: "Not really involved, Charley. She talked to Shad Adams, the feller who killed young Wilton, is all. That's not real involvement."

"Talked to him!" exclaimed Miflin. "She's more'n talked to him, Jess. Those two are going buggy ridin' this evening. She told me that over breakfast this morning. Now, Jess, I want you to do something . . . run Adams out of Singing Springs or. . . ."

"I can't run a man out of town just because you don't figure he ought to talk to Angie, Charley. You know that."

"Jess, you listen to me. If that gunfighter fools around with Angie, I'll break his neck with these two hands."

Jess looked down at the shorter, much thicker man. "Don't try anything like that," he murmured. "Adams may strike you as just another gunman, Charley, but he isn't. He's got a personal feud goin' with the Wiltons. Stay out of his way until this thing is settled one way or another."

"And what about my Angela, Jess?"

Wright slumped. He looked past Miflin's lifted, worried countenance into the brightening roadway. "Yeah," he whispered. "What about Angela?" He brought his gaze back. "All right, Charley, I'll keep an eye on her, too. But you could help by keepin' her busy at home."

Charley nodded, and stepped back out on the plank walk. His smithy was only a few doors south from the jailhouse. "I'll do everything in my power," he said very earnestly. "Thanks, Jess."

Up the roadway Buster Hilton was standing out front of the Cinch-Up. He was smoking a cigar and languidly eyeing the town. Across from the saloon and southward stood Brigham Pruett, also gazing around. When Fred Huff strolled forth from the Mexican's café, both Hilton and Pruett turned so as to watch the Texan. Huff undoubtedly noticed this, but he paid no attention to either Pruett or Hilton. He stepped down into the roadway sunlight and started for the livery barn.

Jess dryly told himself Huff wanted to know whether Shad Adams had returned to town yet or not. Some muffled curses from inside his cell room propelled Jess outside and on over to the café where he got two trays of food and went back with them to feed his prisoners. He'd gone through the stacks of Wanted posters earlier and hadn't found anything that he could be certain pertained to those two, so, when he shoved the trays under the door, wooden-faced he said: "Boys, sometimes it's helpful to be tough and sometimes it isn't. Ordinarily I can't hold prisoners in here any longer than overnight without a signed complaint against 'em, and so far no one's showed up to sign anything against either of you, so I reckon I should turn you loose."

"Then quit preachin' an' unlock the damned door," growled Scar-Face.

"Be glad to . . . the minute you tell me how many men are with the Wiltons and when they'll hit Singing Springs."

"You," snarled the other outlaw savagely, "can go straight to hell. We don't know anyone named Wilton."

"Then," stated Jess, "make yourselves real comfortable because you're likely to rot here."

"You can't do that. You just said no one'd signed . . ."

"I know what I said," interrupted Jess, as he heard his roadside door open and close. "What I *didn't* say was that I can sign those complaints."

"Yeah," cursed Scar-Face. "On what charges? All we were doin' when you snuck up behind us. . . ."

"Carrying concealed firearms," said Jess. "Disturbing the peace."

"What peace were we disturbin', damn you!"

"Mine. Add to that swearing at an officer of the law."

"That's no crime, you . . . !"

"It is now. I just made it one." Jess went to the doorway and looked back. "Think it over. And one more thing . . . make that food last. I forgot to tell you . . . we only feed once a day in this jail."

As Jess walked into his office, turned, and locked the cell-room door, his two prisoners roared hair-raising threats and oaths at him. He straightened up and turned. Fred Huff was leaning against the inside front wall, softly grinning.

"You hit a raw spot, I'd say, Sheriff. What'd you tell 'em?"

"Nothing much. I just sort of implied that they were too fat and needed a one meal a day diet until they decided to open up a little." Jess strolled over, hung up his key ring, and faced the Ranger. "Shad back yet?"

"No. Thought maybe I'd ride out and look around a little.

He's been gone all night, which isn't unusual. Still, I'll feel better riding out than hanging around this town of yours doing nothing. And something else, Sheriff. Singing Springs is getting almighty quiet and funeral-like. You been out this morning? Walk up the road and look at the faces you'll pass. Hell, it's like somebody opened Pandora's box, and what jumped out was something all these folks knew some other time in their lives."

"That's close," murmured Jess, taking up his hat and crossing to the doorway. "I think that's probably damned close, Ranger. Come on, I'll ride with you."

Huff pushed off the wall, left the office, and thoughtfully watched Jess close and lock his office door. As Jess turned, Huff said: "Is that wise, Sheriff? I mean, it might be better if you stayed in town. Time is running out for Singing Springs, you know."

"I won't be gone that long. Anyway, I've got a powerful yen for some fresh, country air. You only know one side of this thing, Ranger . . . the Wilton side. With me, it's different. I know the side you don't even see . . . the side that touches the lives of the folks hereabouts."

Huff shrugged, sucked his teeth, spat aside, and started up along the sidewalk with Jess, toward Sam Potts's barn. Three cowboys entering town from the east boisterously laughed over something one of them had said. Up in front of Hilton's saloon three men were mildly arguing about something. Over by the general store some women were intently talking, their shopping baskets slung from their arms. A wide-tired desert freight wagon was grinding slowly southward down the broad roadway, making ranch rigs and riders give way before it. In front of Pruett's shop an old man was sunning himself, and the heat hadn't risen to its towering fierceness yet, but it was beginning to make itself felt.

Bald Sam Potts was out front of his building, mopping his shiny dome with a limp neckerchief that was none too clean, and a hundred feet northward his hostler was humping up and down as he laboriously pumped the public watering trough full. That trough, punky, water-logged wood, leaked in a dozen places making a splendid green scum around its base where mud-daubers flittered endlessly and where dogs came pantingly to lap up water when the heat was at its wilting height.

Potts turned and gazed at the pair of approaching lawmen. He waggled his head dispiritedly. "Dog-gone hot to be ridin' out," he said, then called to his hostler; although he had nothing to do and could just as easily have gotten the horses himself.

"Gerald, fetch the sheriff's critter an' this other gentleman a horse, too. Step lively now."

Huff gazed around. "Peaceful," he murmured. "Sure a peaceful little town."

Potts put his shrewd, hound-dog eyes upon the Texan and grunted. "Yeah. I reckon hell was peaceful, too, until the devil arrived."

Huff's eyes puckered with sardonic amusement. "The heat's about the same, too," he said to fat Sam Potts, "and the lay of the land. Maybe you've got something there, friend."

Huff stepped around Sam to get into some shade. Jess walked into the barn, too, but for a different reason. He'd just sighted Angie Miflin coming southward with her father's dinner pail, and he didn't want to have to talk to Angie right now. He couldn't exactly define what he felt toward her except that it was a little like resentment. If he didn't have enough hanging over his head, Angie Miflin had to go make eyes at Shad Adams, get her pa all upset, and directly drag herself and everyone close to her into this approaching nightmare with the Wiltons.

"Pretty girl," murmured Fred Huff, watching Angie walk past. "Isn't that the one I've seen Shad talking to, Sheriff?"

"Yeah. Come on, let's help with the saddling." Jess said this so curtly that Huff and Sam Potts both looked at him as he turned and stamped on down where the sweating hostler was hard at it.

Sam lifted fat shoulders and let them drop. "It's the heat," he philosophized. "That, an', of course, them Wiltons."

Huff murmured—"Sure."—and went on deeper into the barn.

They left the livery barn by a back alley, riding due west. For the first hour it wasn't bad, but after that the heat became a curse and a scourge. Even the rattlers they passed were in shade, and, where a lizard panted or a Gila monster lay somnolently, there was a hot haziness.

Farther out there was a blue-blurred smokiness that seemed to dissolve distances, to merge with the brassy sky, and deliberately to appear sometimes as cool shade or running water.

"Like West Texas," said the Ranger. "Hot enough to fry eggs on the rocks."

But Huff, like Jess Wright, was a born and raised Southwesterner. This heat might wilt others, might make travelers ill or listless or frantic to get clear of the desert, but those two passed along through it watching the land for movement, or flashes of reflected light off metal, or anything that might indicate that they were not the only humans out here this deadly time of day.

They saw nothing.

Jess led the way into a deep, crumbly erosion arroyo sixty feet wide and thirty feet deep, cut into the desert floor by some ancient flash flood. There was a lukewarm spring down here beside a paloverde tree where they could water the horses and sit a while. He and Huff had barely dismounted when the Texan threw up a hand for silence.

A rider was approaching from the blurry west and obviously he hadn't seen them enter the arroyo.

Chapter Seven

It wasn't Shad Adams, who both Huff and Wright expected as they stealthily crawled up where they could lie belly down and look over the lip of their secret place. Whoever he was, he seemed uncertain and edgy. He halted his horse a quarter mile out and sat there, testing the air while he very carefully looked out and around.

He was a young man, somewhere in his twenties, although it was difficult to say just where. He had black hair, a broad, flat-featured face, and his coloring was even darker, more oily, than was usual this time of year in hot New Mexico. He was armed with the customary Winchester in his saddle boot and the usual six-gun in its scratched old leather holster along his right hip. But he also had a horn-handled knife on the left side of his shell belt.

"Wiltons aren't very particular," whispered the Texan. "Renegade 'breed Indian, that one."

The rider swung as though he'd heard, which of course he hadn't, and he gazed over toward the arroyo for a long time before looking due eastward in the direction of Singing Springs again. He was riding a fine big blood-bay colt built for speed and stamina, the kind of saddle horse Westerners looked at with the same appreciation they also gazed upon pretty women.

"Anybody you know?" asked Huff.

Jess shook his head. The cowboy looped his reins and began rolling a smoke. As he lit up and snapped the match, he twisted around and looked to the northwest with a particular intentness, almost as though he'd heard something. Finally he took up his reins and eased out, angling on eastward toward Singing Springs, but also riding slightly southward.

Huff grunted, struck at the loam adhering to his shirt front, and turned to slide down where their animals were pleasantly drowsing in paloverde shade beside the spring. By the time Jess got back down there, too, Huff had come to several conclusions.

"Wilton's sent out a scout. That means he's close by. Probably off in the direction that 'breed looked longest. It also means none of what we figured was wrong. He's coming. He's going to risk getting caught by a posse to avenge Johnny."

"What posse?" asked Jess, shaking his head. "No posse's going to trail the Wiltons this far south of Tucumcari, Ranger."

"Don't you bet any money on that, Sheriff, because I happen to know there's a U.S. marshal and a professional posse of damned good manhunters trailing the Wiltons. I beat 'em because I took the stage, but don't think they won't be showing up."

"They'd better hurry," muttered Jess, and went over to get his horse. "Because that half-blood was sent down here to study the land, like you say, which means we can expect to get hit maybe this afternoon, maybe tonight, or, by my calculations, tomorrow at the very latest."

"Which way now?" Huff asked, also mounting up. "We got to keep an eye peeled for that 'breed behind us, too."

"Due north," said Jess, leading the way up out of their arroyo in that direction. "I'm gettin' a little worried."

"About Shad Adams? Me, too."

They rode slowly, raising no dust, and they rode as forewarned men would ride, with their eyes never still. But Jess knew the desert. Northward lay a lot of buckled, broken country which might be ideal for an outlaw band to hide in, but no man, outlaw or otherwise, would deliberately ride through that tortured, broken, twisted land if he didn't have to. They wouldn't want to. They'd want to be able to see all around, which they couldn't do in the brakes.

They were a half mile into the scrub-oak and sage-clump cluttered gullies and brakes when Huff picked up fresh horse sign and pointed it out to Jess.

"One horse, one man," said Huff, and looked up through the breathlessly stifling gully into which this track disappeared. "Shad. Come on."

They rode for almost an hour before those tracks began edging toward the easterly rims of this badlands country. Jess thought, considering Adams's route and the careful way he'd been riding, that he'd seen something. Huff listened to this hypothesis and nodded. Then they came to the farthest reaches of the badlands where the slopes tapered gently up toward the desert's customary flatness and found where Adams had tethered his animal, taken his carbine, and crawled up a slope to lie on his stomach looking westward. They even found where his Winchester butt plate had made its perfect imprint in soft earth, and where Adams's boot toes had also pressed in.

But there was now nothing to see. It was either too heat hazy or what Shad had been spying on was no longer out there, so they retraced their way back a short distance, picked up the tracks where they turned southward, and trailed them until, with the lemon-yellow sun directly overhead, even their horses were beginning to suffer. It was by then at least one hundred and fifteen degrees.

Jess was coming near a gradual lift that would put them back upon the desert floor when, up a gloomy little brush-choked draw, he caught a quick flash of movement from the edge of his eye. He hauled back with his left hand to stop his horse and flashed for his .45 with his right hand. Huff, twenty feet behind, did neither of those things. He simply dropped from his saddle like a stone and swung the animal across his body.

A dry, slightly hoarse voice said—"Hell!"—with such monumental disgust both the sheriff and the Ranger ceased moving. Shad Adams stepped out of the underbrush looking, not at the lawmen, but at the broad, partially concealed rump of his horse. It had been the lazy flicking of the horse's tail Jess had seen. As he turned, his carbine held slanting upward across his body in both hands, Adams swore again in the same disgusted, irritated tone.

He stepped clearly into view, grounded the carbine, and leaned upon it, putting a caustic gaze on Huff and Jess Wright. "You two. That dog-goned horse would have to wag its tail."

Jess slowly unwound, put both hands atop his saddle horn, and gazed disapprovingly downward. "If you'd had any sense, you'd have led him farther into the brush," he growled, nettled at this meeting, at the way it had occurred.

Fred Huff strolled around his horse. Fred had his six-gun palmed. Now he holstered it, wagged his head, and blew out a breath. This meeting had been a very close thing.

"Saw you two trailing me," said Shad, removing his hat to mop sweat off his pale forehead, then replacing the hat. "Didn't figure it'd be the law, and decided to nail me a couple of curly wolves."

"If they hadn't nailed you," said Huff dryly. "Where the hell you been all night?"

"Watching the Wiltons." Shad thrust his chin out. "They were camped in the most northwestern gulch of this broken country. When I found the place yesterday evenin', I figured it'd be a natural hide-out for 'em . . . and it was."

Jess stepped down, looked at Huff, and looked back at Adams. "Did you know there's one of them south and east of here?"

"The black-lookin' one?" said Adams, with a curt nod. "I saw him leave camp just at daybreak this morning. The others left a little later."

"How many?" Huff asked.

Adams turned toward the Ranger, his expression sardonic. He hung fire a moment over his answer, then said with hard bitterness in his voice: "Fifteen, Ranger. Frank, Lance, Stub, and twelve more. The hardest, meanest-looking bunch of brush-poppers you ever saw. Got enough guns amongst 'em to satisfy a small army, and they're mounted on top horses."

"It took you all night and up until noon today to find that out?" asked Jess.

"Sheriff," said the bounty-hunting cowboy, his voice turning flat, hostile, "there's only one way a man alone can hope to hurt a gang as big as that one. No, it didn't take me all night and half a day to figure that out. But it *did* take me that long to crawl around 'em an' see if maybe with a lot of luck I couldn't stampede their horses . . . set 'em afoot. You understand?"

Jess fought down his own hostility with a strong effort. He glared at Shad Adams, thinking of something Fred Huff had said, something about Adams's working very hard to make folks dislike him. Ultimately he said: "All right, you failed."

"Yes, I failed," snarled the lanky, handsome younger man. "But at least I *tried*. I wasn't hobbled to any desk back in Singing Springs like you were."

"Shad," broke in Fred Huff quietly. "Get the bow out of

your back. We're on the same side in this thing, an' you'd better remember that, because if you pull another dumb stunt like tryin' to beard the Wiltons all by yourself, you're goin' to pray you've got a few friends who might save your bacon. Do you know what they'd have done to you if they'd caught you? I mean, especially to *you* . . . bad enough you've been a burr under their blankets since your brother got killed . . . *because you're the man who killed Johnny Wilton!*"

Adams sighed as he gazed from Jess to Fred Huff. He looked hostile, but more than that he looked disgusted. "Come on," he eventually growled. "Let's get to hell back to town."

He turned and went after his horse. Huff walked on up to Jess. They exchanged a dry glance, and Huff shrugged. "I wish I was twenty years younger for ten minutes, Sheriff. I'd bang that damn' fool's head into the sand until he cried uncle."

"Yeah. And you figured him right, Ranger. He sure works hard at antagonizin' folks. Well, like he said . . . let's head back."

They rode up out of the badlands, struck the desert floor with the sun beginning to slide off center, and rode along southeastward toward Singing Springs, keeping a close watch all around.

Adams told Jess and the Ranger that the Wiltons had headed due east toward the stage road that curved in a long arc from north to east, leaving Singing Springs in the direction of New Castle, forty miles away. For a while none of them openly commented upon this, but each drew his own conclusions about that. Clearly Frank Wilton, the brains of the outlaw band, had decided that since his dead brother and his dead brother's companion had entered Singing Springs from the west, the townsmen would be watching for the rest of the gang to arrive also from that direction. They'd figuratively have their backs to the east, and because of this the Wiltons would hit Singing Springs from that direction.

Jess had another thought. "Suppose they put another couple of their boys on a stage like they did the two we've got locked up," he said to Fred Huff. "They could be in town right now."

Huff gazed at the sun to gauge the time. "They could've," he agreed. "Shad says they broke camp early this morning, so they could stop the stage easy enough. Only I don't think Frank'll try that one twice."

"He won't know we got those other two."

Huff lowered his perpetually narrowed eyes and gave Jess a close, shrewd look. "Don't bank on what Frank knows or what he can figure out, Sheriff. Yesterday you were wonderin' how the Wiltons have managed to stay alive this long. Well . . . that's how. By having a feeling about things. Those two like as not were supposed to ride back last night. They didn't. Frank'll scent trouble out of that."

Shad Adams, silent up to now, said: "You're right, Ranger. But what's this about capturin' two of them?"

Huff explained about that, then he dryly said: "You're slipping, Shad, and this isn't a game you can afford to make those mistakes in. Those two would have back-shot you sure as I'm over a foot tall."

Jess, watching Shad's face, saw a faint scowl come and go, almost like a small cloud passing across the sun. Then Adams looked up and caught Jess watching him and turned away.

Jess said: "Adams, you were supposed to go buggy ridin' last night."

Shad swung back around, his dead-level gaze hardening toward Wright. "You got a long nose, Sheriff. For health's sake you'd best keep it out of my business."

Join the Western Book Club
and GET 4 FREE* BOOKS NOW!
A $19.96 VALUE!

Yes! I want to subscribe to the Western Book Club.

Please send me my **4 FREE* BOOKS**. I have enclosed $2.00 for shipping/handling. Each month I'll receive the four newest Leisure Western selections to preview for 10 days. If I decide to keep them, I will pay the Special Members Only discounted price of just $3.36 each, a total of $13.44, plus $2.00 shipping/handling ($19.50 US in Canada). This is a **SAVINGS OF AT LEAST $6.00** off the bookstore price. There is no minimum number of books I must buy, and I may cancel the program at any time. In any case, the **4 FREE* BOOKS** are mine to keep.

*In Canada, add $5.00 shipping/handling per order for the first shipment. For all future shipments to Canada, the cost of membership is $16.25 US, which includes shipping and handling. (All payments must be made in US dollars.)

NAME: _____

ADDRESS: _____

CITY: _____ **STATE:** _____

COUNTRY: _____ **ZIP:** _____

TELEPHONE: _____

E-MAIL: _____

SIGNATURE: _____

If under 18, Parent or Guardian must sign. Terms, prices, and conditions subject to change. Subscription subject to acceptance. Dorchester Publishing reserves the right to reject any order or cancel any subscription.

"That happens to be part of my business," replied the lawman, slightly nettled. "The way I see it, you'd better do one thing or the other, Shad. Not try an' do both of 'em at the same time. And if it's the Wiltons you want more'n Angie, why then don't get her hopes up, because, if you get killed, she's going to suffer."

Shad started to answer that. His eyes were bright with anger, but he checked himself, looked away, and rode along until Singing Springs was in sight before he spoke again. Both the older men were also silent. They concentrated upon studying the roundabout dancing land, for somewhere, perhaps not too far away, was the wraith-like heavily armed half-breed.

They didn't see him, though, and they thought because this was so that he hadn't seen them, either. Fred Huff began to relax a half mile out. He poked along under the blasting, brassy sun with both hands atop the saddle horn, eyeing Singing Springs.

Jess also considered the town. He could see dust rising up from the main roadway where unsuspecting cattlemen came and went. It occurred to him to visit the stage office and Pete Odell's place to see who got off the noon coach, if anyone had.

They entered town from a crooked, meandering little back roadway that led them on in eastward until they hit the alleyway leading to Sam Potts's livery barn. There, at long last able stiffly to dismount inside out of the midday scorch, they encountered the hostler, who looked big-eyed at the dusty threesome, took their sweaty animals without a word, and led them away.

Jess said: "Come down to the jailhouse, you two. I want to have a little palaver with you. And Adams, I want you to look at those men down there, see if you recognize either of them."

Chapter Eight

It was slightly less hot in Sheriff Wright's office than it was out in the shimmering roadway, since at least there were no direct rays to wilt men inside the office. Huff helped himself to a drink from Jess's earthen, hanging *olla,* and remained behind in the office while Jess took Shad Adams in to view the prisoners. When they returned and Huff looked up inquiringly, Jess shook his head to indicate that Adams hadn't recognized his would-be assassins.

Pete Odell, who had seen the lawmen and Shad Adams walk southward from Potts's barn, came shuffling over, his round, sweat-shiny face sharpened by curiosity. Before Pete got his mouth open, Jess asked him about passengers off the midday coach.

Odell shook his head. "Nary a soul," he stated. "Just the usual other stuff . . . the mail, some newspapers, and a couple of bundles for the general store. But Jess, there's something else. A dark-lookin' feller stopped a pair of cattlemen south of town, askin' questions."

Huff and Wright perked up. "What kind of questions?" asked the Texan.

"Like whether the sheriff was in town today, an' if those cowmen had seen the killin' in the roadway, stuff like that."

"Pretty bold," said Huff, turning half around to face Jess Wright. "When we saw that 'breed, he was actin' as edgy as a coyote."

Odell paused, then said: "And he also said there was a feller named Shadrach Adams around Singing Springs, an', if folks knew what was good for their town, they'd run him out."

Jess crossed to his desk, dropped down, and pushed back his hat. He was eyeing Odell pensively. Finally he spoke: "That would've been a couple of hours back, Pete. Since then you've had plenty of time to talk around town."

Odell looked furtively at Adams, and dropped his gaze. Jess didn't wait for the rooming house proprietor to say anything after he saw that look. He kicked the chair around and back again. Odell had talked to Hilton, to Pruett, probably also to Sam Potts, and anyone else he'd run into about Shad Adams.

"Pete," he ultimately said, in a quiet tone of voice, "Mister Huff and I saw that dark-lookin' cowboy, too. Only we thought he was only supposed to scout the countryside. Seems Frank Wilton had something else in mind besides just scouting . . . seems he had in mind getting the men of Singing Springs divided against one another, using Adams and the fact that Adams killed Johnny Wilton. Well, let me tell you something else you can pass around, Pete . . . the Wiltons are going to hit this town like a cyclone whether Shad Adams is in it or not, and don't you ever figure otherwise. They've got that kind of reputation."

Odell gazed at Jess, slowly nodding. "You didn't have to preach me that sermon," he said. "That's what I told the boys. An' we also figured the Wiltons'll be waitin' to see whether or not we run Adams out."

Huff snapped his fingers. "Be damned," he said suddenly. "I never thought of that. They rode east toward the stage road, Sheriff, remember?"

"Yeah. What of it?"

"They'll leave someone up there to watch the road out of town for Adams."

Jess gazed at Huff for a silent, long moment before pushing upright out of his chair. Shad Adams saw that look, guessed how the sheriff was thinking, and stepped between those two lawmen.

"Don't try it," he said sharply. "If you think I pulled a blunder last night, what you two're thinkin' right now will be an even bigger one. You ought to know better, Huff. They'll be expectin' something sly. If you try slippin' out and capturin' that feller . . . or those fellers, dependin' on how many they've got out there watchin' the stage road . . . the rest of 'em'll see you ride out, and they'll hit this town like a herd of war whoops."

Pete Odell, lost in all this, went over to lean against the front wall and perplexedly scowl. Huff and Jess pondered Shad's words. One thing was now uppermost in all their minds: the Wiltons were closing in.

Buttressing his earlier statement, Shad said: "If there was gunfire up along the stage road, the others would hear it. They'd get behind you, cut you off from getting back to town, and your friends hereabouts could bury you . . . *after* the town'd been pillaged and burnt."

Northward, up the roadway, a man's irate voice rang through the thin, hot afternoon. Jess stepped to the door and glanced out. As he turned back, he said: "Just a freight outfit coming down from the north. It crowded some cowman's wagon and he cussed a little at the freighter."

Odell stepped to the door, and also looked northward. Afterward he didn't return to his former place in the office, but stepped out onto the sidewalk. "Got work to do!" he called to Jess. "See you a little later."

No one inside heeded Odell's disappearance. Fred Huff strolled across to a chair and wearily sank down. Jess stood over by his littered desk, faintly scowling. It was Shad Adams who broke the long silence. He addressed Jess Wright.

"Looks like a bunch of cowmen are in town this afternoon. You're going to need every gun you can get."

Adams didn't elaborate. He didn't have to. Jess nodded. If the Wiltons struck in broad daylight, there'd be enough guns around, but the cowmen drifted on back to their spreads around supper time, which wouldn't leave the town in too good a position for defense if the Wiltons struck after dark.

"What'd you think?" he asked Fred Huff. "When'll they likely attack?"

"All I know about that, Sheriff, is that Frank's a smart man. He'll figure to hit you when you're least able to fight back."

"In the dark, then," Jess muttered, and turned to leave the office. At the door he twisted. "Adams, you stay in town. No more playin' Indian."

Shad nodded without speaking.

Outside, afternoon was beginning to spread its thin, hot shadows along the east side of the buildings. There was no coolness in this shade, but it mitigated the eye-hurting sting of the sun's fierce rays, which was something men and animals could be grateful for.

Up in front of Buster Hilton's saloon stood an even dozen saddled horses. That high-sided freight wagon was drawn in snugly at the plank walk's edge in front of the general store, its team of lead horses drooping in their chain harness, and behind them, evenly spaced, stood four more teams, but these were floppy-eared, razorbacked mules, tougher than horses and sometimes smarter than some men.

Jess walked northward. As he was passing the saddle shop, Brigham Pruett stopped him. Pruett was lounging in the weak shade of his open doorway.

"You fellers found Adams, I see," said the saddle maker,

his gray gaze soft and knowing.

Jess halted, nodded, and wondered how Pruett had known he and Huff had been worried about Adams. But he didn't ask that obvious question for two reasons: one, it wasn't important now, and two, he'd come to accept Brigham Pruett's sometimes uncanny ability to guess what folks were up to without ever speaking to them.

"And what else did you find, Sheriff?" the shock-headed big man asked quietly. "The Wiltons?"

"Didn't see them," replied Jess. "That is, not all of them. But we saw a scout they sent out, and we know where they've been holed up."

"Then they're definitely coming?"

"They are."

"Sheriff, Odell and I talked this afternoon before you came back. We didn't know who'd get here first, you or them. So, we sort of took it upon ourselves to pass along the word among the men folk to keep a few guns handy."

Jess turned as two gruff-talking teamsters came out of the general store across the road and crossed to the freight wagon's chained-up tailgate where they went to work. As he turned back, he glanced low and saw the worn, shiny leather of a hip holster peeping out from under Brigham Pruett's wax-shiny work apron. Pruett saw that glance, slowly lifted the apron and disclosed the holstered .45. Two things about that weapon struck Jess Wright at once. The holster, although old and shiny from wear, was a cut-away, the kind of holster only professional gunmen wore. The other thing he noticed was that Brigham Pruett's six-gun had no hammer. Someone had filed off the dog so that only a flat sliver of steel remained. The gun couldn't be fanned, but neither could its hammer catch on a man's shirt, and this was definitely the mark of a gunfighter.

Pruett dropped the apron. His face was expressionless, but his eyes, gray and as steady as rock, showed that he knew how Sheriff Wright's thoughts were running. He said quietly: "You said if I ever wanted to talk, you'd be around. Well, I haven't always been a harness maker, Jess. I went to Mexico twenty-two years ago from Texas . . . with my wife, who was ailin', and my little girl. We had to ride hard. There was a company of Texas Rangers right behind us. Maybe you wondered how I knew Fred Huff. Jess, in all my wanderings I've made it a point to know Texas Rangers. You could almost say I can smell 'em." Pruett's eyes swung away and swung back. "All right, I've talked. There's a heap more, but that's enough. An' after this is over, if Mister Huff comes around, I'll understand. A lawman has to do his duty."

Jess felt ashamed for some reason he couldn't define. He cleared his throat. "Hell, Brigham," he muttered. "Huff's only in Singing Springs because the Wiltons are here. After they leave, why Huff'll also leave. You know . . . twenty-two years is an awful long time. And about your little girl . . . ?"

"She died. She had the lung fever just like my wife. She's been dead a long time. Both of 'em have. When there's nothing left to a man, Jess, why he just sort of drifts along waitin' for his turn." Pruett paused a long time, so long, in fact, Jess thought he was all through speaking. But he wasn't. "One more thing I reckon I ought to tell you. I saw a feller down in Mexico years back. He had a little girl the same age as my little girl was. His wife died, too."

"Sure," murmured Jess, as the realization struck him who Pruett was talking about. "Well, reckon I'll amble on over to Buster's place and see if I can't maybe talk a few of the cattlemen into stayin' in town tonight."

Pruett nodded as Jess moved off. He watched the sheriff all the way across through the light and shadow of the roadway before turning and going heavily back into the quiet gloom of his shop. He'd neglected to mention he'd also had a son.

Buster Hilton saw Jess enter his place and stopped talking to a weather-beaten old cowman with a drooping longhorn moustache, put aside his bar rag, and walked out from behind his counter to meet the lawman halfway. There was slightly more than a dozen idling men in the Cinch-Up, mostly cowmen, but with a few townsmen scattered among them around the room. Hilton looked up at Jess from his swarthy, battered face. "The Wiltons, eh?" he said softly. "We been talkin' about nothin' else in here all day."

Buster Hilton was wearing a tied-down six-gun with a row of crude notches carved deeply into its black, hard-rubber, smooth-worn stock. Jess eyed that gun briefly. He also looked up as all the talk stopped in the saloon. Men were gazing straight at him from the bar, from the card tables, from along the walls where they were standing.

"You fellers know as much about it as I do," he said to all those quiet, stony-faced men. "It's the Wilton gang and they're coming to Singing Springs to avenge the killing of young Johnny Wilton out in the roadway here. There are fifteen men in the gang. There were seventeen, but I've got two of 'em locked up in the jailhouse."

"Fit meat for a lynchin'," that weathered old mustached cowman growled.

Jess let that pass. He eyed the saloon's patrons, and they returned his look stonily.

"They may hit town tonight. I'm asking you boys to stay around tonight and help me patrol the town. Will you do that?"

The men grimly inclined their heads and growled assent. They also made some grisly prophecies and patted their holsters. Buster Hilton turned, went back behind his bar, and began setting up glasses.

"On the house!" he exclaimed. "Belly up, boys, an' drink 'er down." He filled a special shot glass and held it out toward Jess.

The men drank and asked questions. Jess told them all he knew, which wasn't actually much more than they'd already surmised. Then he left them to walk down the east side of the roadway, stopping in the stores to explain what he thought might happen, and finally, down at the rooming house, he ran into Pete Odell, who was also wearing a tied-down gun. Pete colored at Jess's pointed look at that weapon. It was old, with all the bluing worn off, but it rode in Odell's holster as though it had been used a lot and as though it was no stranger to the quick-draw holster.

Jess said softly: "You, too, Pete?"

Odell was uncomfortable under Wright's thoughtful stare. "Me, too . . . what?" he asked.

But Jess didn't explain. He only crookedly smiled and said: "Funny about folks, Pete. I reckon you don't have to ask questions, after all. All you've got to do is wait until something like this Wilton mess comes up, then watch how they wear their guns, and you'll get a pretty accurate idea of how they spent their earlier years."

Odell's color turned bright red. "If you mean this gun," he hastily said, "I bought this off a feller who was ridin' through town a long time. . . ."

"Sure, Pete, sure," said Jess, and smiled. "Forget it. But I'm glad you're on my side."

Jess stepped down into the roadway on his way back to the jailhouse. He suddenly felt warm, satisfied with himself. He'd never been a man to ask a lot of embarrassing questions, especially since they weren't pertinent. Still and all, he had as good a twenty-twenty perception as the next man, and, if he'd been the local lawman all these years in a forgotten little faraway town where a lot of middle-aged gunfighters, outlaws, fugitives had decided to come and settle, it suited him fine, because not only weren't they the least bit inclined to be troublesome, but he had a hunch that like a lot of other kinds of converts, now that they were strictly law-abiding and orderly, they were likely to prove more deadly dangerous to men like the Wiltons than a lot of just ordinary storekeepers could ever be.

Charley Miflin was waiting for him just outside the jailhouse. Charley wasn't wearing his farrier's mule-hide apron now. In its place was a low-slung .45 in a black leather holster. Where the trigger guard lay, Charley's black holster had been neatly cut away so that, in drawing, a man's trigger finger curled around just right even before the gun cleared leather. *Another gunman's trick,* Jess thought, and stepped up onto the plank walk, smiling into Miflin's worried face.

"Come inside out of the heat," he affably said. Miflin stared. Jess perhaps should have looked worried, even distraught, but he didn't. Charley shuffled forward in Jess's wake. He closed the door after himself as though whatever he had to say to the sheriff he didn't want anyone else to hear.

Chapter Nine

When a man hears confidences, he has a choice—he can listen and forget, or he can listen and use them. No man can say it's dishonest if he does the latter, but on the other hand no man of honor can say it's ethical, either. Jess sat in his office with the late-day burnished shadows closing in long after Charley Miflin had departed. He'd been given a confidence. He was still thinking about it when Brigham Pruett opened the roadside door and walked in, looking stern and big, but not especially perturbed, and that proved to be a strongly fatalistic part of Brigham's make-up because he had reason to be perturbed.

"Adams is gone," he bluntly stated, then stood there all thick and oaken, seeing how this information brought a blaze of feeling to the sheriff's eyes. "And that freight outfit that came in town today. . . ."

"What about it?"

"It didn't just have freight in it, Jess."

Brigham held out a big palm. There was a ragged, much-folded square slip of paper in it. "Go ahead," he said, "take it . . . have a look." As Jess obeyed, the saddle maker went right on speaking. "I went over to the general store to pick up an extra box of slugs for m'carbine. This slip of paper was lying in the gutter near the tailgate. I picked it up and opened it like you're doing now . . . then I figured, since it'd obviously been packed around by someone in their pocket for a long time, the teamsters might know."

Jess looked up at Pruett. Stretched before him under his

smoothing hands was a worn, old Wanted poster with a man's likeness etched upon it. "And . . . ?" coaxed Jess.

"The swamper said he didn't know anything about that piece of paper, but the freighter knew . . . I walked him into a dog-trot, Sheriff, and sort of leaned on him a little." Brigham pointed at the face on that Wanted flyer. "He brought that man into Singing Springs in his freight rig. He also brought another feller. Claimed he met 'em walkin' along afoot on the north stage road, felt sorry for 'em for havin' to walk so far during the heat of the day, and innocently picked 'em up."

"Innocently," Jess murmured, tapping the Wanted poster. "It says here one Hank Butler is known to be a member of the Wilton gang."

Pruett gravely inclined his big head. "Both of them are members of the Wilton gang, Sheriff, and they gave that lousy freighter fifty dollars to hide 'em under his goods and fetch them along to Singing Springs."

"Where are they now, Brigham?"

Pruett didn't know. "The freighter let 'em off at the edge of town. I figure that flyer got rubbed out of Mister Outlaw Butler's hip pocket as he was sliding over the tailgate. Anyway, however Butler lost that thing, he's somewhere in town with his renegade pardner, and it's no accident they're here, Sheriff."

"Sure not," Jess agreed quietly, and carefully put the wanted poster atop a stack of similar flyers, stood up, and reached for his hat. "They'll be here to kill Shad Adams, probably. And maybe after that to fire the town."

"After midnight'd be the best time to fire the town, Sheriff. Folks respond poorly after they've been asleep, and a town as tinder-dry as this one is after our long summer would burn to the ground in three, four hours, water brigades not-withstanding."

"You've been doin' some speculating, I see," said Jess.

Pruett looked the lawman straight in the eye as he gently shook his head from side to side. "No, not particularly. But I've seen a town like this pillaged and burnt to the ground, Sheriff. I know what it's like. Let me tell you . . . the screamin' of trapped folks in houses and afterward the stink of burnin' meat never leaves you . . . not even when you're asleep."

Pruett turned, and went over to lay a big paw upon the door latch. He had his back to Jess and didn't face around. "I told that freighter if he was in town come sunset, I'd kill him."

"All right," said Jess.

"We've got to find this Butler feller and his pardner, Jess. We've got to go through town and look in every attic, under every hen roost. We've got to find him an' the sooner the better." Pruett paused, let go the latch, and now turned. "Don't send anyone after Shad Adams. The Wiltons will be expectin' that. They'll be waiting."

"They'll kill him by inches, Brigham."

Pruett remained grimly adamant. "I know that, too, but they'll do the same to whoever goes out after him. Jess, for the town's sake . . . find those other two first. Think about Adams afterward."

Jess considered this, recognized that Pruett had clearly defined the course of his sworn duty. That didn't make him feel any better, but on the other hand he'd told Shad Adams not to leave Singing Springs. A man, especially a lawman in a crisis, could do just one thing at a time.

"Adams will have to wait, Brigham. You're right," he conceded. "About this Hank Butler and his pardner . . . you take this side of the roadway, I'll take the other side. Get the men alerted, be sure they're armed, then let's turn the town inside out until we find. . . ."

"You'll have to get someone else, Jess. I can't work with you. I got something else to do. But I'll be back to join the search as soon as I can. Sam Potts'll be a good man, or Pete Odell or Charley Miflin or Buster Hilton, or those cowmen loungin' around across the way. Only find those two. It won't matter who you use or how they go about their searching. All that'll matter is that those two are found . . . just find 'em, Jess." Pruett reached behind himself, opened the office door, nodded curtly, and stepped out into the reddening afternoon.

For a moment Jess stood looking over where the saddle maker had been. Clearly, Pruett was up to something. He'd never, to Jess's knowledge, been a smiling or easy or relaxed man, and, while Jess now understood what it had taken to change him forever away from warm affability . . . or thought that he did . . . he couldn't recall ever seeing Pruett quite as bleak and seemingly agonized as he now obviously was.

Jess went to a wall rack, selected a double-barrel, half-length shotgun which was loaded with turkey-shot, large, round lead slugs, and put a few extra cartridges in his pocket, still thinking about Brigham Pruett.

He needed Brigham Pruett. He needed every experienced gun hand he could muster. Yet he'd made no attempt to interfere when Pruett had said he had something to do. He couldn't explain, exactly, why he hadn't dragooned the big, shock-headed saddle maker, except to tell himself that it had been because of the raw anguish lying low in old Pruett's eyes. Jess, at thirty-five, had lived long enough in a savage environment to recognize stricken hurt in others. Whatever it was that Brigham Pruett had to do was for their common good, but more than that it was also part of some secret vindication Brigham Pruett now sought, and no man had a right, even under these circumstances, to oppose another man's heart-felt duty.

He went out into the glowing afternoon half light, noticed that the big freight wagon was no longer across the road at the general store, and started toward the Cinch-Up Saloon where the cattlemen were congregating.

Pete Odell saw him stroll past with that riot gun riding loosely in the crook of one arm. Pete looked over where Miflin and Sam Potts were talking in front of the livery barn. Those two also noticed Sheriff Wright with that scatter-gun. They immediately stepped down into the roadway and began angling along behind him. Pete Odell also struck out for Buster Hilton's place.

Others began drifting gravely up toward the saloon along both sides of the roadway. Mostly these were the cattlemen, but there were also a number of armed townsmen, some looking slightly ludicrous with belted six-guns and also gaudy shirt-sleeve garters or sun visors or neckties. The town wasn't doing any business at all now. It was as though some blight had come with the blood-red setting sun. There were no women shoppers passing in and out of the stores. The hitch racks were mostly empty. Here and there a wagon or a top buggy stood deserted at the roadside, but otherwise, excepting the vicinity of the Cinch-Up Saloon, Singing Springs was very hushed, although down both plank walks men were hurrying to the saloon.

Just before Jess entered the swinging doors, he encountered Fred Huff. They exchanged a look, a grave nod, but neither of them had anything to say to each other right then. They entered together. Jess glanced around, and the dozen or so dusty, tough, and quiet cattlemen gazed back. Buster Hilton was at his bar, looking grim. Jess nodded and crossed to the bar. Buster made no move to offer him a drink. Instead, Hilton leaned over his bar top with both elbows hooked there.

It was deathly still in the saloon as more men shuffled

inside. Fred Huff had taken up a position along a wall, and leaned there.

Jess settled back, still with the riot gun in his arm. "Two of the Wilton gang slipped into town this afternoon in a freight wagon," he quietly told the assembled men. "It's anybody's guess why they're here, and my guess is that they came probably to bushwhack Shad Adams, the man who killed Johnny Wilton. It's my second guess they're here to fire the town . . . probably after nightfall. Boys, we've got to find those two men, and we've got to find them fast." Jess paused, looking into all those familiar faces, waiting patiently for understanding to soak in. Only the Texas Ranger seemed neither surprised at Jess's revelation of infiltration nor particularly worried about it.

"How'll we know 'em if we find 'em?" a cowboy asked.

"Any strangers'll do," responded the sheriff. "If you find the wrong men, don't worry about it. We'll lock 'em up until this thing blows over, then turn 'em loose."

This rough, back country procedure seemed to please the men. One of them, a tall, thin, bushy-headed range man, chewed thoughtfully on his tobacco cud for a moment, then said: "Sheriff, you got any suggestions about how we do this searchin'? I'm a mite skittery 'bout bustin' into someone's house and rummagin' around. I've heard tell men've been shot for a lot less'n that."

"Explain why we're searching. No one wants to see their home, their store, or their town burned to ashes. I know the folks hereabouts. No one's going to oppose you . . . mostly, I reckon, folks'll jump in and help. Just be mannerly . . . but find 'em. Hunt those two down like they're calf-killing wolves. But don't harm them. We need all the information they've got."

Jess paused again, considered the men, selected Pete

Odell and Sam Potts to lead the searchers on their respective sides of Singing Springs' wide and dusty roadway. He then turned and told Buster Hilton to take four or five of the local townsmen and search every outbuilding, every hay shed and hen house out back of town. Buster nodded, removed his apron quietly, and hiked on out from behind his bar.

The searchers began to split up. They made a throaty sound with their questions, their curses, grim prophecies, and their back and forth calls to one another as they began moving back out into the dying day.

Fred Huff waited until most were gone before approaching Jess with a mirthless little dour smile making his lips droop. "Odell tell you about those two, or was it Miflin?"

"Neither. It was the saddle maker."

"Oh, yes," breathed the Ranger, his tone scarcely audible. "Brigham Pruett . . . the man with the fine big front window."

Jess looked sharply at Huff, but the Ranger's face was a mask that very effectively hid his thoughts as he returned that look. During the ensuing period of silence between them came the sounds of the searchers passing down through town from the north. Evening would arrive in another hour. The men seemed imbued with an urgency as though sensing a need to finish their manhunt before darkness came.

"One of them is named Hank Butler," said Jess. "Ever hear of him?"

Huff pursed his lips, squinted, and slowly inclined his head. "Bad *hombre*. Who's the other one?"

"Don't know."

"And that freighter . . . what'd you do with him?"

Jess shrugged. The freighter was gone. Whether Pruett had done the wise thing, or the legal thing, in allowing him to go, didn't seem important right now.

Huff saw that shrug and turned toward the door as

Charley Miflin came charging in with a wild look on his face. The blacksmith spotted Sheriff Wright at once and swung swiftly toward him, words bursting past his stiff lips. "Angie's gone, Sheriff. My little girl's gone!"

Both Huff and Wright stared. Miflin's anguish was glaringly obvious even in the late-day gloom. Jess felt a big muscle somewhere behind his belt buckle roll up into a painful knot. Shad Adams was gone, also. Jess forced his voice to be very calm as he said: "How do you know she's gone, Charley. Maybe she's at one of the stores or out visitin', or. . . ."

"Read this!" exploded the agitated blacksmith, pushing a wilted paper at Jess in a shaking hand.

It was a poignant little note from Angela telling her father that she'd seen Shad Adams go out of town, that she'd saddled her horse to go after him to persuade him to come back and stay in Singing Springs because of the terrible rumors she'd heard concerning the Wiltons. Jess handed the note to Fred Huff without a word. That ache in his stomach acquired a fresh painfulness. Charley Miflin's eyes were wild and his lips were gray. He seemed to Jess to be on the verge of some kind of seizure. He said again, in a tone so low it was barely audible: "My little girl's gone . . . she's out there with those men somewhere."

Fred Huff's expression didn't change one whit. He handed the note back to Miflin, reached up to re-settle his hat, and he gave Jess a slit-eyed look. "Keep searching," he said quietly. "And keep Miflin in town if you have to lock him up or knock him over the head. I'll find Angela."

Huff started across the room. Charley Miflin suddenly turned, grabbing for the Ranger. "I'll go with you," he gasped, and Huff knocked him senseless without a word, then passed out of the saloon.

116

Chapter Ten

Jess was still working over Miflin some five minutes later when he heard a gunshot south of town, and after that solitary explosion the quick, high tonguing of many men suddenly excited and agitated. He started quickly to rise up, and Pete Odell came bursting into the saloon. Pete skidded to a panting halt at the sight of Miflin, lying there.

"What is it?" Jess rapped out. "Where'd that gunshot come from?"

"We got 'em!" exclaimed Pete, jerking his eyes off Miflin. "They were on my side of the road down among those adobe *jacales* that're deserted south of town. They're holed up. Couple of the boys started poking around outside an' a couple started to go in . . . somebody in the dark threw a knife and cut Bill Swanson pretty bad in the shoulder. We run up when Bill staggered outside cussin'. We ordered 'em to come out. I came a-running up here for you. I don't know about that shot, but you'd better come right along, Jess, if you want 'em alive. The boys're pretty worked up."

Jess stepped over Charley Miflin on his way to the door. As he brushed past Odell, he said: "Take Charley down to the jailhouse and lock him up, Pete."

Odell's brows shot straight up. "What? Charley? Are you sayin' Charley Miflin is on the Wiltons' side?"

"Hell, no, of course not. But Angela's gone and he's about half out of his head to go after her. We've got enough men beyond town where the Wiltons can kill them. Now you pack Charley down an' lock him up."

Jess hit the plank walk, whipped southward, and began trotting toward the increasing sound of angry voices well below the business section of Singing Springs. He knew the temper of those townsmen and cattlemen, particularly the cowmen. Bill Swanson was a likable cowboy. If whoever was inside an old abandoned adobe shack south of town hadn't tried to kill a cowman, perhaps the other range riders would have been willing to sit out a surround, but not now. Fired-up range riders were often unreasoning, and at any time, when they were mad, they were deadly. He wanted those two renegades alive, not dead.

Somewhere, eastward, a horseman broke into a sharp lope and went clattering northward up through an echoing back alleyway and on out of town. Jess heard that sound, speculated very briefly upon it, decided that rider had to be the Texas Ranger, and kept on until he could see moving shapes on ahead.

The tumble-down shacks south of Singing Springs had, many years earlier, belonged to the large Mexican population which had formerly lived on the old-time contraband route into and out of their home country, but for at least a quarter of a century now these thick-walled little mud houses had been used only by occasional destitute range riders on their way through the country, or until, if they were the lucky ones, they found work on the cow outfits beyond town.

The house Jess saw all those angry armed men surrounding was slightly apart from the other adobe *jacales*. It hadn't appeared to suffer from neglect as much as most of the surrounding shacks had. Its windowless wall openings, small and placed high so that prowlers would be discouraged as well as its doorless front opening were heavily recessed in the stout, baked-earth walls. Even the roof still retained its sharp erectness against the darkening sky of pre-evening.

Paul Kandelin, the stage line representative in Singing Springs, walked up to Jess with a long-barreled Springfield Army rifle in his hands and said: "I been tryin' to tell 'em it might be just some strange cowboys in there, or maybe scairt Mexicans, Sheriff. You better take a hand. They're gettin' ready to rush the place."

Jess moved around Kandelin, saw Buster Hilton vigorously arguing with a crowd of angry men, and hastened forward. Hilton saw Jess and turned indignantly to say: "All right, you bunch of damned idiots, here's the sheriff . . . let's hear what *he* thinks about charging that cussed house!"

There were at least twenty men out there, and, as they moved aside so that Jess could get up to Buster Hilton, they disclosed an injured man seated in their midst atop a rusty bucket. He was stripped to the waist, splashed with blood, and several other cattlemen were bandaging his right shoulder. This was Bill Swanson. He looked up at Sheriff Wright and made a small, self-conscious smile, although his cheeks were gray.

"There's two of them in there," Swanson said in reply to Jess's lifted brows. "I saw that much before someone flung that damned knife and hit me in the shoulder. I never got a chance to open my mouth and neither of them said anything, either." Swanson flinched as the bandage was made fast, licked his lips, and said: "It's darker'n the inside of a boot in there, Sheriff, an' those two'll fight . . . whoever they are."

Hilton said stiffly: "Might not even be the right men, for all we know. Hell's bells, if a bunch of men as raunchy-lookin' as this crew busted in on me while I was sleepin' in a deserted shack, I reckon I'd get a mite upset, too, Jess. Tell these wild Injuns to stand back . . . let's you 'n' me try talkin' to those fellers in there."

Jess had already made up his mind about this, so he now

nodded, and at once all that discordant, angry talk dwindled
down to a long, pregnant silence. Jess beckoned the men back
away from the house. They came reluctantly, particularly two
range riders who had gotten up against the windowless back
wall. Both these men gestured protestingly with their drawn
guns and walked away disgustedly only after Jess insisted
upon it.

Then Jess called out: "You fellers in the *jacal* . . . walk out
the front door without your guns!"

There was no movement, no sound, from the mud house.
Where the red-flashing sun was sending its dying rays against
the *jacal*'s front and north walls, the building looked rusty.

"Listen!" Jess called again, his voice sharpening this time.
"I'm Sheriff Wright of Yaqui County. Come out and you
won't be hurt. If you *don't* come out, we'll smoke you out.
Now make up your minds one way or the other."

Jess had scarcely stopped speaking when a ray of scarlet
light flashed upon a gun barrel in the east window. Men broke
and scattered in all directions. Even wounded Bill Swanson
went over backwards off his rusted bucket in a frantic dive
toward safety.

The gun exploded, its red lash of flame making a violent
splash of light inside the house. Jess moved sideways, drew,
and fired. He had no target but that gun barrel, and he missed
that.

Other guns opened up, too. Somewhere northward from
around a neighboring shack, Kandelin's Springfield rifle
made its flat, vicious *crack*. Buster Hilton fired through the
window from his position near Jess, down on one knee. Jess
put up his six-gun, hefted the ten-gauge, and suddenly made
a lunge forward, utilizing all that angry gunfire as a cover to
get up against the yonder wall. At once his companions
ceased firing for fear of hitting their sheriff.

When the last echo died out, Jess raised up a little, holding his shotgun across his body, and said to the men inside the house: "Boys, you made the wrong decision." He then spun around, lifted the shotgun, rammed its snout through the window, and fired one barrel.

The unnerving roaring flash of this most lethal of close-combat weapons on the frontier brought a quick, breathless cry from within the little *jacal.* Jess dropped low and jumped sideways where he flattened back with both shoulders pressed to the warm adobe.

Burnt gunpowder made its pungently wreathing little dirty cloud in the window opening. Facing Jess several hundred feet northward were the others. Mostly they had achieved cover among the other abandoned old adobes. Their faces faintly shown, and their guns, but of their bodies Jess could see very little.

Inside, that same crushing silence ensued. Off in the distant west the sun was nearly gone now. It would remain light for another hour or so, but definitely dusk was approaching.

Jess called out: "Throw out your weapons and walk out of there, boys! You haven't the chance of a snowball in hell." There was no reply to this order. In fact, try as he might, Jess could detect no sound inside the house at all. He thought, only for a moment, that his turkey shot might have had a wide enough pattern to have got both of those protected outlaws. But he thought this only for a moment, because, around by the front door, two guns suddenly opened up with deafening thunder.

Someone cried out in a shocked way from among the other houses, and a man staggered out into plain sight and, dropping his carbine, pitched forward. Buster Hilton was beginning to yell something to Jess when the wrathful offensive gunfire began again. That shot man among the attackers had been seen by his companions and they were enraged all over again.

Their gunfire drove that outlaw back deeply into his little room again. Pieces of ancient adobe flew out of the walls in chunks. Pete Odell appeared suddenly, without a rifle. He ran to the downed man, caught him roughly by both shoulders, and dragged him out of sight around a building.

Jess raised his shotgun overhead, poked it through that window again, and fired the other barrel. As before, that stunning explosion and accompanying blinding flash of light distracted everyone. The gunfire, for a moment, dwindled. Buster Hilton used this moment to spring furiously over and throw himself bodily against the wall opposite Jess. In the failing daylight Hilton's scarred, swarthy face looked evil and murderous.

Jess reloaded, stepped over to Buster, handed him the scatter-gun, and put his head close to the squattier man's ear. "I'm going for the front door," he said. "You keep 'em down with the shotgun."

Buster twisted his mouth to protest, but Jess swung on past, came to the corner, and stepped around it out of Hilton's sight. Now, as before, that fierce gunfire from the attackers died out and a frightening silence deepened.

Jess got right up next to the door and flattened there. "For the last time," he said, "fling out your guns. You've got five seconds to make up your minds, then we're comin' in with shotguns."

For the first time, a man's voice came out of the Stygian blackness inside the one-roomed little *jacal:* "What you want us for? All we're doin' is beddin' down for the night an' all of a sudden there's a stinkin' army outside screamin' to lynch us."

"The guns," reiterated Jess. "Toss out the guns. Then, if

you're what you say, you can keep on riding."

The gruff voice from the darkness said: "All right. Just hold off with that damned blunderbuss."

A six-gun sailed through and fell ten feet from Jess in the churned and dusty roadway. He waited a long time before another six-gun, also, sailed out.

"Now your carbines . . . and knives," Jess demanded.

"Ain't got any," said the gruff voice sullenly. "Had a knife, but when some feller jumped in here swingin' a Forty-Five around, I threw the knife at him."

"Then walk out . . . and be careful, cowboy, real careful. There are close to thirty guns out here."

A man's booted feet shuffled through the darkness inside. They came right up to the door, halted, then minced back and forth as though their owner was strongly hesitant.

Jess said: "Come on. You'll be safe."

The man edged right on up to the door, poked his head out, swung northward, and was staring right down the raised, cocked pistol barrel Jess was holding forth. He blinked and started to recoil. Jess reached out in a flash, caught the man's shirt, and wrenched him out through the doorway. The moment he let this man go, he flung around and ran as fast as he could straight southward. At once several range men dropped their carbines, let out wild whoops, and lit out after him.

Jess stepped five feet to the right, sprang into the blackness within that little house, and dropped down low. No gunshot came.

It was hopelessly dark in the *jacal*. He could not make out where that other outlaw might be, so he spoke to the man. There was no reply. He tried again. Still there was no reply. He cocked his six-gun, felt for a match, struck it, and held it up at arm's length.

Twenty feet away, evidently knocked there by the charge of buckshot that had killed him, the second outlaw sat propped along the south wall, sightlessly staring from wide-open eyes.

Chapter Eleven

Buster Hilton came in after a careful call to Jess. He brought with him a lantern. Other men crowded inside, too, all of them silent the moment they saw that dead outlaw. Buster held his lamp above the dead man, squinting. He shook his head back and forth. He didn't recognize the outlaw.

Jess took the man's guns, rolled him over to locate and remove his wallet, then ordered the closer men to take the body to the embalming shed. He and Buster walked back outside where men crowded around to watch their sheriff go through the dead man's wallet.

There was a little money, a faded, old folded letter obviously read and re-read, and, finally, there was a likeness of the dead man carefully folded and evidently cut laboriously from a Wanted poster.

Buster lowered the lantern as a number of panting men came back to join the others, their faces glistening palely in the sickly light. One of these men said between deep gasps: "They got him, Sheriff. Odell and the others caught him runnin' up the alleyway behind your place. They're holdin' him up there for you . . . in front of the jailhouse."

Jess looked over where two men were coming around from behind a house. That was the identical *jacal* where Odell had earlier dragged the shot cowman. He called over to those men. "How bad is he?"

One of them turned and answered. "We stopped the bleedin', Sheriff. He took one flush across the top of the head. It plowed a neat slit, but he'll be all right after his head

quits achin'. We're goin' after a pony of whisky now to pour
down him."

Jess looked around at the other men. "Go on up to
Buster's place. Drinks are on me. I'll come along later." The
men started breaking up. "And one more thing," Jess called
after them, "there are thirteen of the Wilton gang left, boys,
and they are still dead-set on leveling this town. Keep an ear
to the ground an' an eye open."

Someone chuckled. "Sheriff," this man plaintively asked,
"how you expect a man to drink in that position?"

Buster Hilton blew out his lantern, looked at the dead outlaw's wallet in Jess's hands, and wagged his head as he also
turned and went pacing along northward up toward the
center of town. Jess took his scatter-gun and went on up to
the jailhouse. Odell was there, along with three others includ-
ing Sam Potts who wasn't built for chasing people and who
now loudly gasped as he tried to recapture his normal
breathing rate.

Jess didn't speak as he opened the jailhouse office door
and led the way inside. He turned up the lamp and for the
first time got a good, close look at his prisoner. Despite the
sweat, the dirt, and about six days' growth of peppery whis-
kers, Hank Butler was unmistakable from that Wanted poster
he'd dropped. Jess gazed at him briefly, then motioned him to
a wall bench and turned to the others.

"I'm obliged, Pete, Sam . . . all you boys, for runnin' him
down. He was foolish to think he could get away like that on
foot."

"Desperate," muttered one of the other men, shooting
Butler a dour look.

"Thanks again!" Jess exclaimed. "Up at Buster's place the
other fellers are having drinks on me. If you hurry, you can
still make it."

At once the men stepped over to the door. Sam Potts and Pete Odell were not in that big a hurry, but they, too, eventually departed, leaving Jess and his prisoner alone in the office.

Jess sat upon the edge of his desk after putting up the shotgun. He said quietly to Butler: "That was pretty dumb, sneakin' in like that this afternoon. Why didn't you just wait until nightfall? A whole cussed army could sneak into Singing Springs after dark without being caught . . . if they knew how to do it."

"I dunno what you're talkin' 'bout," growled the outlaw, eyeing Jess coldly. "Me 'n' my pardner was just riding through your country when all of a. . . ."

"Butler," said Jess, leaning over to lift the first flyer off his stack of Wanted posters. "Look."

Butler looked, suddenly reached for a trouser-pocket, then swore with feeling as he guessed what had happened and how. After that he put aside all pretense. "All right, Sheriff, you're right. I'm a Wilton man. So was that feller you killed with your cussed turkey-shot. So was Johnny Wilton, the boy you butchers shot down in the roadway of your two-bit little town. An' every time one of you pulls a trigger, you're just diggin' the grave deeper for every stinkin' man, woman, an' kid in Singing Springs."

Jess kept gazing across at the outlaw. "Finished?" he quietly asked.

"Yeah, I'm finished. Every word is true, too. You'll find out soon enough."

"Got a couple of your friends locked up, Butler. Come on, I'll let you see 'em."

Jess got his keys and took the outlaw into his back room, and the minute Butler saw those other two he swore at them. But those two still, at least for a moment, tried to keep up their pretense. When Butler said—"Frank figured you two bungled it."—the scar-faced outlaw glared at Butler and swore.

"Yeah. *We* bungled it! An' just what are you doin' in here, Hank?"

Jess opened the cell door, gave Butler a rough shove, slammed the door, and locked it. Two cells distant Charley Miflin was gripping his bars with big, curled fists looking pitifully out at Jess. But Miflin didn't say a word until Jess left those snarling, caged outlaws, fiercely arguing now among themselves, and walked on to where Charley was.

"Killed one an' captured one, Charley. Gettin' a fine collection of scum."

"Let me out of here, Jess."

"Sorry."

"How can you do this to me, Jess?"

"For your own good, Charley. Ranger Huff went after her. Shad Adams is out there, too. By now I reckon he's found her. She's got all the protection we can give her."

"Not *all* the protection. Let me out."

"Not until they fetch her back."

"Jess, for Gawd's sake I'm her *father!* She's all I've got in this world. If anything happens to her. . . ."

"Charley, damn it all, I told you to keep her occupied, to keep an eye on her." Someone entered the outer office and slammed the roadside door hard. Jess broke off talking and started on to the cell-block entrance. Charley Miflin called out something muffled to him in an unmistakably desperate, reedy tone. Jess kept right on going.

The newcomer was garrulous Paul Kandelin from the stage line office. Paul was still carrying his Springfield rifle. As Jess came along, Kandelin pushed out a hand. He had a note which Jess took, opened, and read. All through this neither he nor Kandelin spoke.

The note was from Buster Hilton. It said simply that Jess should come at once, that north of town there was a fire visible, east of the stage road. Jess put the note upon his desk, puckered up his forehead, and quizzically gazed at the stage line manager. Kandelin spread his hands.

"Some of the boys say it's the Wiltons up to something. I got no idea what the fire signifies, Jess."

"No buildings up there, Paul?"

"Nope. Come on. You can see it easily from the center of the roadway."

Kandelin went to the door, opened it, stood aside until Jess had passed on out, then closed it after himself. Out in the roadway Jess saw the flames. They were rising almost straight up.

"A good mile an' a half out," speculated Paul Kandelin. "There's nothing up there but the road, Sheriff. Aren't any ranch buildings that close to town. What in tarnation does it look like to you?"

Jess didn't reply. He started walking on up the center of the roadway toward Hilton's saloon. There were people standing totally quiet along both sides of the road, also gazing up where those wild red flames stabbed into the darkness far out.

Buster Hilton was with Pete Odell and two cattlemen. He turned, saw Jess and Paul Kandelin, stepped away from his companions, and walked out where the sheriff halted.

"Could it be some kind of a beacon, Jess? Could the Wiltons be signalin' friends to come join 'em in the attack on Singin' Springs?"

Jess shook his head. The fire was big, and it was bright, but neither Fred Huff nor any of the outlaw prisoners he now had, in all their threats and other talk, had mentioned any available outlaw reinforcements for the Wiltons, and he was very certain that, if such help was available, his prisoners wouldn't have neglected crowing about it.

"Then what's it mean?" Buster asked, turning to face northward again.

There was, in Jess's view, just one thing that it *could* mean. Since it would require a lot of work to gather dry brush, tumbleweeds, dead cacti to feed that fire, and, since it served no purpose at all up there in the middle of nowhere in the night, it had to be designed to do precisely what it was now doing, getting all the attention of Singing Springs' residents turned northward.

Jess looked over where the cattlemen were standing, all bunched up in perplexity near Buster's saloon. Elsewhere, up and down the plank walks, armed men stood gaping.

"Buster, take the cowmen and get around behind town to the east. I'll gather up some townsmen and patrol the west. I'll tell you what I think that fire's for . . . it's to divert all our attention northward while the Wiltons hit us from another direction."

Kandelin jumped like he'd been stung. Hilton's puzzled expression slowly changed. He abruptly turned and walked back over to where Pete Odell and the cattlemen were standing.

Jess heard him bark at those men in short, savage sentences, but Jess didn't wait for any more. If he was right about that fire, and, if it had been burning very long up there, then it was perfectly logical to assume that the Wiltons were right this very minute skulking just beyond town out in the night.

He went hurrying along the west side of the boardwalk, calling to men to fetch their weapons and come along with him, and finally the spell that mysterious fire had caused was broken. Men began running back and forth, joining one posse or the other, all of them carrying rifles or carbines or shotguns, and within moments, as this fresh preparation for battle got under way, the few women who had also been silently lining the roadway disappeared.

Jess wasn't aware of Paul Kandelin, trailing along beside him, until with some sixteen or eighteen men he got to the westernmost reaches of town and paused to have the men scatter out.

Paul said, a little breathlessly: "Maybe some of us ought to walk out a ways, Sheriff, an' try to spot 'em before they get in close." As he said this, Kandelin was standing in the reflected orange lamp glow of a nearby house, holding his long-barreled Springfield in both hands.

From the darkness in the west a Winchester made its savage, throaty roar, and Paul Kandelin gasped, put forth a hand as though reaching for support, then fell to the ground with a little rustling sound.

Men cried out anxiously. Most of them were already fanning out among the buildings. They had seen that muzzle blast out there in the night, and they had heard the explosion, but had not been able to see Kandelin fall.

Jess bawled at them all to take cover, that the Wiltons were out there a hundred yards in the moonless night. As the others called back and forth Jess got hold of Kandelin, dragged him behind a shed, and knelt over him.

Kandelin was dead.

East of town there were several quick, flat gunshots, then a quick bawling of breathlessly inquiring voices. Jess looked over in that direction. He had full confidence in Buster Hilton's ability to guard that side of town, but what he wondered, kneeling there beside the dead stage company executive, was whether those shots had killed any more of his defenders.

A hundred yards south of Jess two townsmen suddenly

fired. A ragged flash of answering shots came back from the night-shrouded desert. Jess got up, and started northward. His defenders were entirely alerted now. If the Wiltons had planned on catching Singing Springs unawares by employing that bonfire as a ruse, by now they should realize they'd failed.

Chapter Twelve

It was an eerie, unreal fight. The darkness was total, men had only very brief glimpses of their targets, and the gunfire was sporadic. Sometimes twenty minutes would go by without a single shot being fired by either side.

Buster came trotting over in search of Jess. When they met, Hilton shook his head. "Like Injuns!" he exclaimed. "They're tryin' all kinds of tricks. Sometimes they sneak up and try belly-shootin' from the ground. Sometimes it's little flurries by five or six of 'em. Jess, we got 'em outnumbered. Why not get set all together an' charge 'em?"

"Lose men that way, Buster. We've got to do it their way. We can't let them get close enough to fire the place. My guess is that's what they're planning. We're just damned lucky we figured out what they were up to before they got in." Jess paused. "They got Paul Kandelin."

Buster looked down through the back alley where he and Jess were standing. His swarthy, tough-set face looked unrelenting in the gloom. "I told you, Jess," he mumbled. "I told you they were bad clean through." He shot a swift glance upward. "Pete told me about Charley's girl and Adams. I've never been a prayin' man, but I could sure pray right now."

A fresh, brisk exchange of gunfire broke out southward behind the jailhouse. Both Hilton and Sheriff Wright turned to watch those venomously winking flashes of lethal red light out there. The townsmen were reinforced from both sides, and the outlaws were finally driven back.

Jess hefted his Winchester. "You better get back with your

crew," he said. "That Texas Ranger said Frank Wilton's the brains of the gang. If he's very smart, he's going to figure out pretty quick now that he's not strong enough to fight past our boys. Buster, he'll try some trick or other. You better be over there and ready when he does."

Hilton nodded and swung away. Jess started on down the alley moving from shadow to shadow, from shed to shed, until he was even with the livery barn. There, he encountered Sam Potts's wispy little hostler, quaking like a leaf in a wind storm, but resolutely guarding the doorless back opening into the barn.

"Watch close!" called Jess, and kept on moving.

A man spied Jess and grinned, his white teeth making a bright splash in the otherwise dark face. Jess smiled back. Not that he felt the least like smiling, but because, as long as local morale was that high, he'd do nothing to dampen it.

He went past where Paul Kandelin was cooling out and eventually arrived behind the jailhouse. There, two crouching men told him that several outlaws had attempted to rush them. "Probably figured them other scum are locked up," one of the townsmen acidly said, "and thought they might get in close enough to set 'em free. Well, we singed their tail feathers a little. They won't be back right away."

Over eastward across Singing Springs' roadway and beyond the yonder buildings a flurry of thunderous gunfire blew up into a head-on fight. Jess and the men around him west of town listened closely to that bitter battle. It was very definitely to their advantage to know whether Hilton's men stood fast or not, because, if the outlaws fought past and got into town, Jess and his men would be flanked between two fires.

But Hilton's roar of profane triumph came eventually to reassure the sheriff and the townsmen. Then there was a long lull before the individual, sporadic sniping began again. What began to disturb Jess was the stubborn persistence of the Wiltons. Outnumbered and exposed beyond town on the flat desert or not, they were returning to the fight. Whatever else they were, Jess told himself, they were not cowards. Of course, the moonless, inky night was strongly in their favor, but it was past midnight now, the town was staunchly holding them back, and unless they could devise some way to get close enough to set their fires soon, within the next two or three hours dawn was going to catch them in the open without adequate cover, and they'd have to withdraw or be killed.

Finally the attackers ceased all gunfire. A tense, deep hush ensued. Jess passed back and forth among his townsmen, telling them not to leave, not to expose themselves or believe for a moment that the Wiltons weren't still out there. He then passed between two buildings, emerged into the empty roadway, crossed over, and turned to step between Odell's rooming house and the general store on his way in search of Buster Hilton, when he heard several quick cries of sharp alarm southward.

At once the gunfire broke out again. It was brisk and ragged as it swelled and ebbed. Jess, surmising what had happened, turned and went trotting down the sidewalk toward the fresh sounds of battle. The Wiltons, using that deliberate lull in the fighting as a ruse to make the defenders believe they might be withdrawing, had instead skulked southward down among the adobe ruins and had crept in quite close to the nearby wooden buildings before they had been detected and fired upon.

As Jess arrived down where the muzzle blasts lanced orange in the darkness, he could see that the Wiltons were in strength here. They fired, darted to different positions among the *jacales,* and fired again. For a bad moment they advanced almost to the edge of town. Jess dropped to one knee at the corner of the closest building and fired at gun flashes. Twice he drew hostile fire, and twice he was driven back to take cover as the Wiltons made their desperate bid to get close. But other defenders, also drawn southward by this concerted push, began to add their flaming resistance, and finally the outlaws, slinking forward, could not advance farther. That was when Jess saw the first fire arrow. It was arced in a high, lofting flight so that it struck just below the roofline of the nearest wooden structure.

Jess recklessly ran over where Buster Hilton had come up with three men, dropped down behind an adobe ruin, and pantingly directed the men with Hilton to climb atop the eastward buildings and stamp out those fire arrows the minute they landed. Those men ran off swiftly. Buster sighted a man lingering around a distant *jacal* where he'd swing out, fire, and swing back. He patiently waited. When the renegade jumped clear, Hilton fired. The outlaw cried out, and collapsed.

There were three men firing those fire arrows. This was Frank Wiltons's newest trick. Jess saw the arrows rise up and loop overhead, but he couldn't locate the bowmen firing them.

Suddenly Pete Odell stood up with a shotgun to his shoulder. Jess and Buster started to call to Odell to get under cover, but the deep roar of Pete's shotgun drowned them out. Jess, gazing skyward, saw one of those burning arrows suddenly burst into a hundred sparks in mid-air and fall harmlessly to earth.

Men cheered, and Pete Odell broadly grinned just before he dropped flat to reload. Odell had shown the defenders how to counter Frank Wiltons's deadly trick. After that, the very second a fire arrow appeared, every man with a shotgun opened up on the fiery object. Eventually, with no fire arrows even getting close to their objectives, and with the cattlemen and townsmen cheering, hooting, and making a game of this kind of shooting, the outlaws stopped trying to set fire to Singing Springs in this manner, and shortly afterward, with others drawn south by the shouts and the gunfire, the Wilton gang was driven back out from among the *jacales* to the night-shrouded, flat desert again. After that, there was another of those long lulls.

Buster Hilton and Jess Wright went back over to the westerly defenders. They were keeping their vigil, but some of the bolder spirits among them were unhappy about not having been able to participate in the south end fight. Buster and Jess told them grimly not to worry. Their turn would come. The Wiltons were not giving up, and every time there was one of these periods of deathly quiet, they could be assured the outlaws were up to something.

Afterward, Buster and the sheriff went along to Sam Potts's barn, stepped inside, and took stock. It was while they were discussing their chances and their defenses that a quiet, lean shadow entered the barn from up front and walked down toward them. Jess looked and thought he recognized that silhouette, and he was right.

Fred Huff came up, grounded his Winchester, leaned upon it, and solemnly nodded at Wright. "Bad night for gettin' any rest," the Ranger drawled.

Jess could make out that Huff's clothing was soiled and stained and disheveled, but it was too dark inside the barn for him to make out the Texan's expression, or, for that matter, his actual features. His face was only a pale blue in the roundabout gloom. Still, there was a slump-shouldered, weary stance, and there was a tonelessness to

Huff's voice showing fatigue.

"Find anything?" Jess asked.

"Only the outlaws, Sheriff," Huff replied. "Ran into them almost head-on before I'd been out of town a half hour. They built that big fire north of town, stoked it good, then split up, one band on each side of town, and went to the attack. I had a devil of a time gettin' through. Bad enough havin' the Wiltons shootin' at me, but when I was between them an' the town, I began to pick up a little lead aimed my way by your boys. Had to belly-crawl near a mile." Huff straightened and cocked his head as a sudden burst of gunfire broke out behind them across the alleyway and among the westerly buildings. When it dwindled away almost as abruptly as it had swelled, he relaxed again and wagged his head. "That Miflin feller I knocked out, is he still in town?"

Jess nodded. "Locked up for his own protection in the jailhouse."

"And those skunks who sneaked into town in the freight rig?"

"One's dead with a load of turkey-shot through him. The other one's locked up. The live one is Hank Butler."

Huff digested this, then he looked at Hilton and Wright. "I never saw hide nor hair of Shad Adams or the girl. But I *did* catch a glimpse of a big, bare-headed man astride a black horse."

"Pruett," murmured Jess.

Buster Hilton started. "Brigham Pruett, Jess? You mean he's out there *with* them?"

"Among 'em, maybe, Buster, but not with them. He left town before they lit their bonfire."

"What in hell did you let him go for?"

Jess and Fred Huff turned at the sharp, breathless tone Hilton was using. They stared even though they couldn't see that Hilton's dark and swarthy countenance was screwed up into an expression of bitter denunciation.

"What's on your mind?" asked Jess. "Buster, is there something wrong . . . something I ought to know?"

Before Hilton could respond, Fred Huff said: "I thought, when I spied that feller, it might be your friend Pruett. I can tell you this much. He was stalkin' the Wiltons like a strong-hearted Apache buck." Huff looked squarely at Hilton. "I don't know what you're worryin' about, mister, but I'll tell you this . . . if I was Frank Wilton, I'd worry a heap more about havin' that feller behind me, than I'd worry about havin' you and all your townsmen in front of me."

Hilton subsided. His dark eyes glistened in the gloom as he stared hard at the Texan. In an altered, almost subdued voice he said: "Maybe you're right at that, Ranger. Maybe . . . well, never mind."

Jess, on the verge of asking a question, didn't get the chance. Buster said—"Better get back to my boys."—and abruptly walked toward the front of the barn.

Jess scratched the back of his neck. He and Fred Huff traded a look.

Huff said: "I think they'll get him, though. He wasn't makin' any effort to hide himself from the Wiltons."

Jess, recalling the way Pruett had looked and acted the last time they'd been together, puckered his eyes in thought. "He's a good man, Ranger. Pruett's a good man. Singing Springs could use a couple dozen more just like him."

Huff didn't answer. He took up his carbine, dropped his face to examine it, and afterward walked back into the alleyway. From there he said softly: "Sure quiet, Sheriff. Too quiet. They're up to something."

Jess walked out back, too. He halted, lifted his head, and sniffed. Dawn wasn't far off now. One thing about the summertime desert, it had no secrets, if a man knew how to detect them, like scenting the coolness, the acrid fragrance that invariably preceded the dawn.

Men moved here and there among their defenses. An air of relaxation seemed abroad now. There had been no gunfire for almost an hour. Some of the cattlemen who'd been in that fire arrow attack down among the *jacales* strolled over to exchange experiences with townsmen on the west side of Singing Springs.

The sheriff called out a warning for the men to keep their sharp watch, then he and Fred Huff struck out for Jess's jailhouse where Wright had a fire-blackened old graniteware coffee pot of generous proportions that he put on his little potbellied stove, and stoked up a fire beneath it.

Huff settled his weary frame in a chair, leaned aside his carbine, and put down his hat. It was dark in the office. Jess, for obvious reasons, made no attempt to light a lamp. As he took a deep drink from his *olla,* those three incarcerated renegades beyond the cell room door began to call out. Jess ignored that, crossed to his desk chair, and dropped down.

Huff's strong, even teeth showed across the gloomy little room in a humorless smile. "Singing Springs wins the first round," he murmured.

Jess nodded. "Who'll win the second?" he asked.

Without any hesitation Huff said: "If I was an impersonal bettin' man, Sheriff, I'd lay my money on the Wiltons. They know now they can't outfight you . . . and you've got to stay right here in your town and wait for whatever they'll try next. That gives them a big edge."

Chapter Thirteen

Dawn came. People, at first with great caution but after a while quite boldly, stepped out into the roadway and paced along the sidewalks. There was no sign of the outlaws, and excepting for Paul Kandelin's body, having been borne to the embalming shed by his friends, some broken windows, and a lot of fresh gouges where bullets had struck, Singing Springs didn't seem changed a whole lot.

Northward, a lazy cloudiness hung in the still morning air where the bonfire had burnt down to ashes. There was an unmistakable stench in the clear air of burnt gunpowder, but as the morning advanced, even this faded away.

The sun glided steadily up toward its zenith on its east-to-west crossing. It piled up the heat, leeched all moisture from the early morning coolness, and eventually Singing Springs was well into another fiercely hot and wilting midsummer day.

"It's unreal," Sam Potts told Jess and Fred Huff as the two lawmen encountered Sam over at the Mex Café where they all ate breakfast. "They're still out there somewhere. You can't see 'em, but you know blamed well they're out there. Hell, we don't even know if we killed any of 'em. They're like Injuns . . . they packed away their dead . . . if they had any dead."

"They had 'em," Huff stated dryly. "But it's the live ones I'm concerned with, not the dead ones."

Sam dabbed at his unnaturally high forehead and watched their food come as he said: "Sheriff, how come y'don't make

141

up a posse and go run those fellers clean down into Mexico?"

Jess answered shortly. "An' strip the town of men, an' maybe the Wiltons get around me and come back? Sam, as a livery man you're tolerable . . . as a lawman you'd be pretty sorry. Eat your breakfast."

They ate. Some cowboys stamped in to eat, and at sight of the Texas Ranger and their sheriff they made a few crowing remarks. They were in high spirits.

Jess ordered four trays that he and Fred Huff returned with to the jailhouse where three were given to the outlaws while the fourth was pushed under the door of Charley Miflin's cell. Miflin pleaded with Jess to be set free, but all the outlaws did was curse because it had been so long between meals.

Buster Hilton and several of the cattlemen drifted down to the jailhouse about ten o'clock. The cowmen were impatient and said so.

"Who isn't?" Jess demanded of them. "You got some idea I enjoy sittin' here?"

"Then why are you doing it?" a cowman asked gruffly.

Jess explained again about what could happen if he left Singing Springs with a posse in search of the renegades. Buster Hilton was nodding his head before Jess had finished speaking, but then Buster had just lately become a very staunch supporter of the sheriff.

That restless cowman then said: "Sheriff, we got ranches and families an' herds an' buildings that also got to be protected. We can't hang around town forever."

Fred Huff, sprawled in a chair across the room, said dryly: "Want to bet? Boys, you're not leavin' Singing Springs until this is settled one way or the other. As for your ranches . . . don't worry about them . . . the Wiltons are strictly town raiders."

A doleful-looking older man gazed evenly across at Huff. "Who says we're not leavin' Singing Springs?" he demanded. "You, Ranger?"

"No, pardner, not me. The Wiltons." Huff waved his hand in a circular gesture. "They're out there, watching every trail an' every road. Go ahead, if you're that foolish, an' try it. They'll have your scalp within two miles."

The cattlemen looked at one another. Buster Hilton, leaning upon a wall, gazed at Jess and shrugged. He didn't say anything.

Fred Huff stood up, mightily stretched and mightily yawned. He was watching those ranchers in a patronizing way. They seemed uncomfortable and looked over at the sheriff, who only nodded at them. Finally they left the office.

Buster didn't depart with them. "I figure we got to bury Kandelin this morning," he told the lawmen quietly. "Too hot to put it off very long. Want me to take care of it, Jess?"

"Be obliged if you would," stated the sheriff, and walked to the door, pushed it wide open, and leaned in the opening, looking up and down the shimmering roadway. "How's the feller who got creased over the head, Buster?"

"Mad an' a little shaky, but otherwise all right."

Hilton stepped through the doorway, paused outside to look up and down, then he said: "What'll they likely try next, you reckon?"

Jess shook his head. He didn't know. Behind him Fred Huff looked like he might have an idea along that line, but Huff kept still. This wasn't his town; it wasn't even his fight except insofar as the Wilton brothers were concerned. He sat back down and went to work manufacturing a smoke.

The morning wore along. Occasionally townsmen or cowmen drifted by for a brief conversation, but mostly the pair of peace officers was left alone. At high noon Jess returned to the doorway, stepped out, and leaned against an upright post of the overhang, gazing northward. Huff joined him.

"Figuring the stage driver might have seen something?" he asked quietly, and Jess nodded.

But the noonday stage didn't arrive in Singing Springs.

Sheriff Wright and Ranger Huff walked along to the late Paul Kandelin's office and met the little stage line crew up there. The freight clerk said dolefully: "It's usually late, Sheriff, but not *this* late."

The swamper who was also the mechanic in the same funereal tone said: "They done stopped it out yonder somewhere, Sheriff, sure as the devil. Singin' Springs is cut off just like us folks here in town don't even exist."

Jess and Fred Huff sauntered back outside beyond earshot of Kandelin's stage line employees. "They're probably right enough," admitted Huff, gazing into the heat-blurred northward distance where the roadway shimmered and writhed. "At least as far as stoppin' the coach is concerned. What I'm wondering about, Sheriff, is that posse."

Jess nodded. "I was wondering the same thing, Huff, until a little while ago. Now, I think they probably turned back and gave it up."

Huff immediately disagreed. "No, sir. Not on your life. Like I told you, Sheriff, these men aren't a lot of cowmen or clerks . . . these are professional manhunters. They don't give up an' turn back."

"No? Not even when they know that by now, if the Wiltons had kept going, they'd be safely over the line down into Mexico?"

"Not even then, Sheriff!" exclaimed Huff adamantly.

Jess had his strong doubts, but he let it lie there. It wasn't important, anyway, he thought, because whatever the

Wiltons had in mind, they'd do before the posse men could arrive. Then he heard the faraway, familiar sound of chain harness, steel tires rattling over summer-hard ground, and finally, only half believing his ears, he and Huff both sighted the spiraling cloud of dust where the south-bound stage was whipping along.

Huff said—"I'll be damned."—and sounded nonplused.

In front of Hilton's saloon several idling, dour-faced cowmen strode out into the roadway to crane northward. One of them whooped, and within seconds people, both men and women, rushed forth to line the roadway on both plank walks. It seemed as though that oncoming coach held some key to survival for these people, while actually, in Jess Wright's view, it was nothing more than the daily coach arriving late.

Finally, when the rig was fully in view, it slowed to a trot and approached Singing Springs with the horses catching their wind from a long run. By then it was obvious to all the smiling, laughing, immensely relieved onlookers that both the driver and his shotgun guard were atop the box and that nothing untoward had occurred. But they were wrong.

Jess and Huff, already standing before the stage line's Singing Springs office, simply waited. But other people, as the coach ground into town, hastened up to meet it, to wave their hats and call greetings to the brace of stony-faced bronzed men up there on the box. When Jess saw how those two gazed unsmilingly at the townsmen, he let off a resigned breath, straightened from the post he'd been leaning against, and said quietly: "Ranger, the Wiltons have made their move."

Huff didn't comment. He resettled his hat lower over his eyes to protect them from the trailing gray cloud of dust, hooked both thumbs in his shell belt, and stood motionless until the driver eased in at the curbing, halted, and hurled his ribbons to the waiting swamper who would make the team exchange and grease the wheels before the coach continued on its southbound way again.

The bronzed pair on the high seat got stiffly down. Neither of them cast more than a cursory glance at the beaming townsmen who were crowding up as they reached the roadway, but both of them saw Jess Wright and converged upon him. The whip was a wispy, graying man probably in his late forties or early fifties. He was a thin-lipped, humorless man with eyes the color of smoke on a wintry day. He strolled up in front of Jess, plucking off his gauntlets. Without a word or a nod he pulled a slip of paper from his belt, held it out, and said shortly: "Careful how you open it, Sheriff."

Jess looked from the driver to his shotgun guard. Both men were bitter-eyed and grim in the face. He opened the paper carefully. There was a lock of soft-curled fair hair folded into the note. He recognized that hair at once. So did some of the townsmen peering around his elbow and across his shoulder. A quiet, shocked little sigh ran over the crowd.

There was a line of heavy scrawl underneath that golden lock of hair, and a bold, black signature. Fred Huff bent his head, read the note, re-read it, then straightened up. Jess also read the note. It said only that Angela Miflin was in the hands of the outlaws, and that they wouldn't harm her until sundown, providing that Shadrach Adams was sent to them in exchange for her. It was signed: **Frank Wilton**.

Huff didn't look as stunned or as pained as Jess and the others around him who'd read those words. He and the stage men exchanged a solemn glance.

"Where'd they stop you?" Huff asked.

The shotgun guard, in the act of handing his weapon to the company's freight clerk, looked around. "About two, two an' a half miles north. Up where the road curves off in the direction of New Castle."

"How many?"

The guard shrugged. "Only two. If there'd been more, we wouldn't have stopped . . . we'd have made a runnin' fight out of it. I think they knew that, so there was only two of 'em."

"You ever seen those two before?"

The guard shook his head.

Buster Hilton pushed out of the crowd behind Jess, his swarthy, scarred face smooth and wire-tight. To the driver he said: "Sam, was *she* with 'em, by any chance?"

The driver turned, spat, turned back, and replied: "No, Buster. It happened just like you guys just been told. Two of 'em signaled us an' we stopped. They handed us that there note, said . . . 'On your way . . . just remember, after sundown, we'll send the girl back to you instead of just a lock of her damned hair.' An' we come on into town."

A tall, dark girl who could have been part Mexican said very softly into the long hush: "Holy Mother . . . !"

Jess held that lock of golden hair between two fingers, the scribbled note in his other hand. He looked a little ill.

A gruff cowman roughly pushed up. "All right, where's this Shad Adams? If he's any kind of a man, he'll ride on out."

Jess said softly: "He rode out last night . . . before the fight. He's already out there somewhere. For that matter, so is Brigham Pruett. They won't know anything about this, an' I doubt like hell that we could find Adams now to tell him."

That cowman's jaw sagged. His screwed-up, little eyes slowly turned toward Jess, hot and indignant. "You let him get away?" he demanded. "Sheriff, just what in the hell . . . ?"

"Easy," said Huff. "Calm down, mister. No one knew this would happen, and Shad Adams went out before we even knew for sure the Wiltons would hit Singing Springs."

"She saw him riding out and went after him," explained Jess, twisting to face those stunned people. "I had to lock Charley Miflin up in the jailhouse to keep him from goin' after her. They'd have killed Charley."

The same cowman looked at the others, then back to Jess again. "Sheriff," he said very softly, "it's after two o'clock right now. The sun'll set at eight-thirty or nine tonight. That ain't much time. Listen, we got to make up a posse and go hunt down this Shad Adams."

Chapter Fourteen

Jess had a hard decision to make, and he made it as soon as the irate cattleman stopped speaking, but he had no intention of concealing the facts, either, so he told the townsmen his private thoughts.

"Listen to me. This talk of a posse going out there is foolish." When that angry cowman would have interrupted, Jess held up his hand. "Just you listen a minute. A big posse might find the Wiltons . . . might even wipe them out . . . but they'd see the dust, and they'd see the men. These Wiltons are anything but just ordinary renegades . . . they're like Indians, only worse. They'll have spies out watching Singing Springs. They'll be waiting for us to make some foolish move now. We beat 'em off last night, in the dark, but today it's different. In broad daylight the odds are even . . . maybe the odds are now in their favor. And one more thing, folks. If I strip this town to get up a posse . . . the Wiltons will be hoping for just exactly that. They'll let us get a mile or two out, then they'll hit this town with bullets and torches. They'll kill the womenfolk and the kids."

Jess stopped speaking. The crowd gravely watched his troubled face for a moment, then turned to murmur back and forth among themselves. He'd driven home his points vividly enough. Even the wrathful cattleman had no more objections to offer.

Fred Huff, who none of these people actually knew except by rumor, stepped out where the stage driver and his shotgun guard were standing, just off the plank walk in roadway dust, and said: "Folks, your sheriff is right. There is one more thing, though. If the Wiltons didn't get Shad Adams when they captured the girl, don't you ever believe the picture's as black as it looks right now. You don't know me an' you don't know Shad Adams, but I'll tell you two things about him . . . he's got an old personal score to settle with the Wiltons. They killed his brother down in Texas . . . and the other thing is simply this . . . Shad Adams is the deadliest man with a gun I've seen in many years as a Ranger going up against fast guns. As long as he's on the loose out there, I wouldn't want to be a Wilton."

"How d'you know they ain't got him, too?" asked a bearded man in the crowd.

Huff wagged his head cynically. "They wouldn't be asking to trade Angela for Adams if they had, or, if they'd killed Shad Adams, folks, they'd be so happy they'd let the world know about it. Remember, it was Adams who killed Johnny Wilton right here in your roadway. No, sir, Shad's still on the loose out there, and it's my guess they don't even know he's on their trail."

"Brigham Pruett, too," said a woman hopefully. "He's also out there, stalking them, isn't he, Sheriff Wright?"

Jess nodded, but he didn't speak. He was running some notions through his mind, and, whatever else was said here, he knew for a fact that it was now no longer possible for him to wait for the Wiltons to come to him to finish this fight. *He was going to have to go to them!*

"Go on home," he said to the crowd. "Go on back to your stores. Leave this to the Ranger and to me."

Jess moved out where Fred Huff stood, took the Texan's arm, and moved off. Behind them the crowd began talking earnestly and excitedly. Huff, taking the pulse of that band of irate people, said: "Sheriff, there'll be some hotheads who'll try sneakin' out of Singing Springs. You can bet on that."

But Jess shook his head. However, they were down near the jailhouse before he'd perfected what he had in mind and told Huff what it was.

"I'm going out there, Ranger. If you want to come along, I'll be right proud to have you, but regardless of that I've got to go out there."

"Well, sure, I'll traipse along," responded the Texan. "That's what I came here for . . . to get a good bead on the Wiltons. But that doesn't solve your trouble with the local folks, Wright."

"I can take care of that, Ranger. Buster Hilton, Sam Potts, Pete Odell, an' a few others can police the town, can make damned sure no idiots try sneakin' out to get themselves killed."

Huff thought on this briefly, found it plausible, and nodded his head. It was then very close to three o'clock in the afternoon. "All right, Sheriff, but just how do you figure even the two of us can get out of Singing Springs without being detected? Remember what I told you about the Wiltons . . . they can out-Indian any Indian. If you figure to ride out, forget it. They'd bushwhack the pair of us before we got a mile away."

"We're not going horseback, Ranger."

Huff's eyes widened. "Afoot?" he said incredulously. "Five hundred lousy miles of desert to get over, and you're thinkin' of tryin' it *on foot?*"

Jess smiled. It was his first smile in a long while. He entered the jailhouse office, beckoned the Ranger in after him, crossed to the rifle rack upon the wall, took down two rifles instead of carbines, handed one to Huff and gestured for the Texan to help himself to ammunition.

"Shoot farther," he said shortly, stuffing bullets into a

trouser pocket. "Sight better with rifles and outshoot anyone armed only with short-barreled carbines."

Huff, filling a pocket with bullets, said dryly: "Yeah, and a hell of a lot more awkward to carry, too."

Jess checked the magazine of his rifle without having any more to say until Fred Huff was ready, then, jerking his head, Jess walked back out of the office after taking down his key ring.

He walked across the road with Huff pacing beside him looking skeptical but asking none of the obvious questions, and entered Pete Odell's rooming house. Pete was standing beside a roadway window, gazing out. He'd seen the lawmen approaching, met them with a quizzical expression, and, when Jess held forth his jailhouse keys, Pete took them.

"Round up Buster and Sam and anyone else you think you'll need," instructed the sheriff, "and make damned sure no hotheads try slipping out of town, Pete. Watch those cattlemen especially. If anyone gives you trouble,"—Jess nodded his head at the key ring Odell was holding—"lock them up."

"Where you two goin'?" Odell asked in a reedy, suspicious tone of voice. "Jess, for gosh sakes don't try anything. . . ."

"Don't fret about us, Pete. You just make damned sure you boys here in town do your part. Huff and I'll worry about what we're up to."

"Amen," muttered the Texan resignedly. "Only I can't worry properly unless I got some idea what we're going to try, Sheriff."

"We're going after Angela Miflin," said Sheriff Wright, and turned on his heel, leaving Odell and Huff standing there, looking nonplused.

Jess was stepping down to cross the roadway before Huff caught up with him. But the grizzled, squint-eyed Texan didn't say a word. He simply trudged on across toward the livery barn. He did not, however, look exactly delighted at what he now knew of Jess's plans.

Potts wasn't at the barn. His hostler said he thought Sam was over at the Cinch-Up where most of the other agitated townsmen and cowmen were meeting. Jess wasn't perturbed by this. In fact, he acted as though he were relieved by not having to face Sam.

"You're going to turn loose ten or twelve head of horses," he told the hostler, and, when that man's eyes popped wide open, Jess added: "Don't worry, Sam'll understand, and, if we don't get 'em all back, I'll stand the gaff in dollars."

"Horses, Sheriff?" whispered the dumbfounded hostler. "What horses?"

"It doesn't matter. Ten or twelve of your least valuable ones. Come on, show us which ones Sam cares the least about."

Jess and Fred Huff started down the wide, earthen alleyway looking at the stalled animals. The bewildered hostler scuttled along after them full of questions and protests. Jess cut him off, finally, down near the back alley entrance to the barn.

"Old horses and unsound ones, critters that, when the Wiltons catch 'em, they won't be able to remount themselves on as replacements for their own critters. You understand?"

The hostler was direct. "No, I don't understand. Sam'll have a fit."

"He'll just have to have it, then. Come on, we don't have a whole lot of time."

Jess sized up several drowsing, stalled animals nearby, selected one particularly aged, sway-backed animal, led it out of its stall, and pointed toward another, equally as worthless, beast for Fred Huff.

"You ride that one," he ordered. "I'll ride this one."

Huff looked at the beast Wright had indicated and made a little sniffling sound. "He can't pack a saddle, let alone pack me, too."

"You won't be ridin' a saddle, Ranger. Neither will I. We're going out of here bareback Comanche-style . . . like side-riders."

Fred Huff finally understood. He said—"Ahhh."—in a long outward expulsion of breath, with his narrowed eyes beginning to show comprehension. "With eight or ten other loose horses runnin' around us. Why didn't you say so?"

Jess didn't answer. He gestured around at other horses. "Cut 'em loose and I'll block 'em at the alleyway door until we're ready," he said to the hostler.

Huff turned. The hostler was looking pleadingly at him as though he'd suddenly become convinced Sheriff Wright was out of his mind. But Huff was no help. He simply made a cruel little grin and said: "It just might work at that. Every now an' then a bunch of horses busts out of a corral. All right, mister, you heard the sheriff. Cut 'em loose!"

The hostler was neither an aggressive nor a very assertive man. He looked around and dropped his shoulders, then began obediently to walk up and down among the tethered horses, turning loose an animal here and another animal there.

As Huff and Jess watched, standing beside their haltered animals, Huff said he thought they'd stand a much better chance of getting far out if they didn't have to hang onto those rifles and the horses' manes at the same time. Jess's answer to this was curt.

"Without a rifle how long would we last?"

Huff said with equal asperity: "Maybe we won't last long, anyway. If we get outrun, they'll see us sure."

The hostler called forlornly from up near the road-side

154

front entrance: "They are loose, Sheriff . . . ten of 'em . . . and, if you two fellers don't make it, Sam's never goin' to believe this story when I tell it to him with no one to back me up."

Jess swung up, reached forward with his left hand to grasp the halter of the horse he was astride, and look across where the Texan also sprang up. Huff's lips were sucked back flat against his teeth. He obviously was beginning to have doubts about this venture.

Jess eased over to block the alley opening. "You ready?" he asked the Ranger.

Huff nodded. "Ready as I'll ever be."

Jess called up to the hostler to push the milling animals along, rode out into the alleyway, and set himself to cut the loose stock off from turning southward. Huff came through, also, and the loose horses began to walk outside into the dazzlingly hot afternoon brightness. At first these animals, finding no guiding hand upon them, were unsure. They milled and sniffed and lifted their heads up high. But when Jess whirled the beast he was riding toward them, they broke away northward, and, after the fashion of all loose horses, the moment they found that no one was going to halt them, they kicked up their heels, rolled their eyes, snorted, and went on up the unimpeded alleyway in a swift rush.

Jess and the Texan struck their mounts and in a flash were in among those running horses. Where they swerved left to leave town, two strolling armed men appeared abruptly in the alleyway's opening, quickly heard the coming stampede, and Jess had only one brief glimpse of the astonished expressions on those two faces before both men whipped about and leaped wildly back to safety. Afterward, riding low over the neck of his excited animal, Jess heard those two townsmen yell in sharp anger.

There were several other fluting cries as the livery animals were seen breaking clear of Singing Springs in a wild and apparently unguided stampede out over the western desert, but within minutes all that was far behind. Jess dropped down low and kept his mount in the middle of that rushing herd. Huff was right behind him nearly enveloped in gray dust. The heat, the thunder of shod hoofs upon iron-like baked earth, the snorting and squealing, all combined to give a very graphic illustration of loose horses wildly running.

For what seemed hours but what was really only a matter of twenty or thirty minutes this wild, dusty charge went on. Jess raised up when he thought it was safe to do so to gauge the swiftness of their passage and the amount of miles covered.

He knew this country inch by inch and, by poking the free-racing animals nearest him, was able to head the whole band over toward the deep erosion gully where he and Fred Huff had rested the only other time they'd ridden out this way together, the day they had been searching for Shad Adams.

They got to that gulch, but as the uninhibited horses flung themselves up and over, and abruptly downwards into that place, Fred Huff lost his hold on the mane of the animal he was astride, struck the ground, and rolled nearly a hundred feet before he fetched up in a catclaw clump.

Jess saw it. He saw, too, that there was no way to catch Huff's mount, get the Ranger back astride, and get any farther along without it being evident to anyone who might be watching that these were not just loose-running horses, so he hauled back on his mount's halter at the bottom of the arroyo, swung his right leg over, released all holds, and landed running as the horse he'd been astride picked up speed and raced away in the wake of the other animals.

Jess went to where Fred Huff was profanely picking catclaw thorns out of his hide. He retrieved the Texan's rifle, wiped it off, handed it to Huff, and smiled. They'd made it!

Chapter Fifteen

"Sorry," growled the Texan, looking out where that little band of horses was laying a dust screen straight northward up alongside the badlands. "My palm got sweaty, an', when the blasted critter swung downhill, it threw me forward." Huff took his rifle. "I lost my hold."

Jess wasn't disturbed. "You hurt?" he asked. "Looked to me like you rolled halfway down the slope."

"I did, but it's crumbly ground. Might be a little stiff tomorrow, but I'm fine right now . . . except for these damned thorns."

They crept to the far lip of the arroyo and flattened belly down, gazing far ahead where the dust from their borrowed remuda looked thin and far distant. The horses had skirted that broken, badlands country, had sped along within a hundred or so feet of the first breaks, going due north in the direction of the Wiltons' previous dry camp.

"No one's after 'em yet," said Huff, intently watching. He then rolled up onto his side, reached forth to part the sage thicket that shielded them, and slowly looked west and south. Jess was coming up into a sitting position off the ground when Huff drew in a sharp breath. Jess swung his head quickly, following out the line of the Texan's vision.

There was a pair of horsemen loping up from the south. They seemed to be very closely watching that distant dust cloud, but the course they were on would take them well around and to the west of the arroyo.

"Sure could use those horses," Huff muttered, straining

toward those two men. Then he swore for an obvious reason. Whoever those men were, they had spotted the arroyo and swung wide to go around it.

Jess was interested in the horses, too, but he was more interested in the men. "If they're part of the Wilton bunch, Ranger, then they'll be the scouts watchin' the southbound trails out of town." He was about to follow out this line of deduction when something a long way down country behind those two flashed dazzlingly for a fraction of a second in the pewter-hot afternoon sunlight, and instantly winked out.

Huff's expression of fierce envy abruptly altered. He had also spotted that wickedly bright reflection. "Someone's followin' those two, Sheriff," he said, "or my name's not Huff."

They let the pair of horsemen lope past and get well northward before leaving their uphill hide-out to return to the arroyo's secluded floor. From here they hastened westerly in a recklessly exposed rush hoping to get up the extreme slope down there where they'd be close enough to spot anyone else following along on the tracks of those two other men.

They made it, got up the crumbly slope, flopped down breathlessly in a clump of wiry sage that flourished near the upper lip of land, and there they waited. There was not another of those telltale flashes of reflected light off metal, and, although they were motionlessly silent straining to pick up the sound of an oncoming rider, they failed in that, too.

Finally, a half hour later, Jess looked around. "If it was someone trackin' those other two, he either changed course or stopped before he got up this far."

Huff growled agreement, swung over onto his back where he had an unobstructed view back down their arroyo, and suddenly went rigid. In a very low whisper he said: "Don't make a sound. Turn around an' look down the draw."

Jess did. Back several hundred feet was a burly, large man on foot crouching over their recently made boot tracks along the arroyo's bottom. He had no hat, but he wore a cut-away gunfighter's hip holster and was carrying a Winchester carbine in one big fist. They couldn't see his face clearly, nor for that matter could they any more than make out that he was tracking them, was tensed up with the knowledge that their boot marks were very fresh. He stepped behind a little paloverde, stepped out again, still tracking them, then he suddenly halted to run a careful gaze on up to the brushy rim where Jess and Fred Huff were scarcely breathing as they watched.

Harsh sunlight struck that whiskery, broad face. The expression was resolutely fatalistic and the heavy features were closed to reason and logic.

Jess let his breath out. "Pruett," he said quietly to the Texan. "If we were the Wiltons, we could pick him off as easy as shootin' fish in a rain barrel." He started to get up.

Huff put out an arm. "Wait a minute, Sheriff. I can see Pruett's face good from here. I think he'd as soon shoot us for tryin' to stop him or turn him back as he'd shoot a Wilton. Better let him go."

Jess bent forward slightly as Brigham Pruett began walking again, alternately gazing at the ground and at the uphill lip of crumbly arroyo bank. He didn't believe Pruett would throw down on him at all, but he never got the chance to prove or disprove this. Northward in the middle distance a man's fluting call floated down the afternoon. Jess dropped flat. So did Fred Huff. They had no time to look back and see whether or not Pruett had also heard that call.

Huff swore and pointed. "Our little scheme backfired some way," the Texan murmured.

There were four riders coming down from the broken

country, riding bunched up and clearly backtracking those loose horses Jess and Fred Huff had utilized to escape detection when they'd left Singing Springs.

Jess watched for a while, then said: "I'll tell you about what's happened, Fred. They overtook the herd and found seat and leg marks on two of the horses."

Huff pushed up his rifle with a bitter little nod. He didn't say anything; he simply squirmed around until he was in a position to drop the foremost of those horsemen if he had to.

The outlaws halted a hundred yards out, spoke a little among themselves, and one man pointed dead ahead. He seemed to be explaining to his companions about the arroyo up ahead. Jess shouldered his rifle. If those renegades went down into the arroyo, they'd not only find where two men had abandoned their mounts and had run over this way on foot, but they'd also stumble onto Brigham Pruett. He twisted to glance back where they'd last seen the saddle maker. Pruett was nowhere to be seen. Obviously he'd also heard those riders coming.

A bad fight was shaping up now. Pruett, down in the arroyo, didn't know who was up above him along the northward lip of land, and it was now too late for Jess and Huff to sing out. If there was shooting, it was entirely possible Pruett would throw some lead their way, too.

Evidently the Texan was thinking along these same lines, for he grumbled: "I'd trade these bushes for boulders right about now."

Some sense of caution seemed to intervene here. The outlaws suddenly split up, two riding straight ahead toward the arroyo's northern lip, the other two heading in a westerly direction, following out the course of the two men who had earlier come up this way from the south.

"It's that same pair," Jess observed, pressing down flatter

because, while the brush around them offered excellent shelter downhill and even northward, it offered no shield at all to the west. He and Fred Huff pushed themselves backwards as far as they dared, seeking to get as much camouflage as possible around them.

"They'll be in range," stated the Texan softly, watching those two renegades as they leisurely came on. "These two don't worry me much. It's the other two."

Jess raised up just enough to get a brief downhill look. There was still no sign at all of Brigham Pruett, and because, wherever Pruett was hiding in the underbrush, he was unable to see up over the northward rim, he'd have to gauge the imminent danger only by sound. On the other hand, as those two outlaws went steadily forward toward the arroyo's rim, their own downward view kept widening and broadening.

Jess had very little doubt of how this fight was going to end so far as who was going to triumph was concerned. He and Huff had greater firepower, and they also, so far at least, had the advantage of surprise. But Brigham Pruett was vulnerable down in the cañon. The two men overhead would undoubtedly be able to see the saddle maker down in the draw before he'd be able to see them.

Jess flattened beside the Ranger and thoughtfully considered the other two oncoming outlaws. They were almost within rifle range now, and Huff was curling his cheek lower over the rifle stock as he tracked them down his long barrel. Jess brushed the Ranger's arm.

"Don't shoot," he whispered. "We've got to get the other ones first."

Fred rolled his head around, looking both irritated and perplexed. He was waiting for Jess to continue, so the sheriff did. He explained Pruett's position and urged the Texan to turn and look for himself. Huff did. For a long moment his slitted eyes and bronzed face were forbiddingly harsh, then he turned back, shrugged, and nodded.

"I reckon you realize," he said quietly, "that the second we open up on those two, the two out front of us are goin' to know right where we're shootin' from. Even if we can roll downhill before they get us, Sheriff, our two will get away to warn the others and fetch 'em back here."

Jess knew this. He also knew, as he twisted to watch the farthest pair of outlaws, that within one minute they'd be directly above the arroyo on its north rim and that somewhere underneath them in the underbrush a man as big as Brigham Pruett couldn't possibly be missed by their rummaging eyes or, afterward, by their bullets.

"It's more important to save Pruett than it is to knock over all four, and, if we can get their animals, we'll get up yonder into the badlands . . . then let 'em come."

Huff turned wry. "Let 'em come?" he said, gazing straight at Jess. "You tired of livin', Sheriff?" Then Huff shrugged, cast a final, unhappy glance out where those two riding outlaws were now well within rifle range, and turned deliberately around to sit with both knees raised. He placed both his elbows on his knees, pushed the long barrel of his rifle carefully through the sage, and grunted. "One thing's sure workin' for us, Sheriff. These here rifles. I guess I got to hand that much to you." Huff looked over to where Jess was also taking a long rest, and made a tough little grin. "Remind me to compliment you on your foresight . . . if we live through this."

Down in the arroyo a thicket quivered. Both the lawmen saw this and knew what it meant. Brigham Pruett had suddenly realized that the outlaws up atop the rim would be able to see him the moment they stepped up to gaze down into the gully. He was frantically trying to make himself less conspicuous.

Overhead, those two horsemen suddenly halted, yanked out their carbines, and swung down. They paused to look right and left, to discuss their strategy, and meanwhile, around to the west, those other two renegades were moving steadily along where they could easily flank Jess Wright and Fred Huff.

Neither lawman said anything. They could see the brush patch where Pruett undoubtedly was, although they could not actually see the saddle maker. They could also very clearly see those two big-hatted, heavily armed, and unkempt-looking outlaws off on their left within rifle range.

One of the outlaws seemed to think he and his partner should split up, should take two different approaches to the arroyo's lip. This man kept gesturing around. But his companion wasn't at all favorable to such a notion and adamantly wagged his head. Evidently this man thought that two guns in a pinch were better than one.

Finally the argument was resolved. The stubborn man had won. Both the renegades turned aside to find brush to tie their horses, then they came together and started on over the last several feet toward the rim.

Without taking his eye off those two, Fred Huff said: "Look around, Sheriff. Can those other ones behind us go into action before we can tumble down off this lip?"

Jess looked. The unsuspecting southward-riding outlaws were directly behind them. They were a hundred yards off, too far for accurate pistol fire but not too far away for accurate carbine fire. As he turned back to drop his head down and draw a bead again, he didn't give Huff a direct reply. What he said was: "Ranger, the second we fire, whether we hit 'em both the first crack or not, start rolling down this damned hill."

Huff gave a little grunt. He understood their peril exactly.

"I'll take the one to the right of us, Sheriff. You take the other one. And, Sheriff, don't miss!"

Over along the northerly rim that stalking pair of outlaws came up almost to the rim. They could not see straight down yet, but they commanded an excellent view of the southward slope and part of the arroyo's floor. There was nothing to be seen of Brigham Pruett yet, which made them bolder. They stepped up the last ten feet, and all hell broke loose.

Fred Huff fired. A fraction of a second behind this initial detonation, Jess also fired. Unexpectedly, from down below where Pruett was crouching in underbrush, another thunderous gunshot flashed redly in the downhill gloom.

Without waiting to eject their spent cartridge casings or reload, both Huff and Wright sprang up, flung themselves bodily over the nearest clump of brush, and went crashing wildly downhill.

They didn't even see one of their victims over on the north rim collapse forward, tumble out over the lip of land, and fall like lead straight down into the arroyo. The other shot outlaw crumpled right where he stood.

Off westerly a man's high, startled yell rang out. That remaining pair of horsemen swung their horses inward, toward the vacated uphill westerly rim, firing six-guns as they charged into the fight. There were no targets for them to aim at, but they riddled the sage clumps.

Down in the arroyo, well beyond where Wright and Huff were frantically plunging, Pruett opened up on the west rim with his carbine. It was this savage gunfire that broke up those two charging horsemen and sent them wheeling back the way they had come. Pruett was standing straight up, half his upper body exposed, as he fired uphill.

Chapter Sixteen

Jess got under cover near a spindly little paloverde, and Fred tried to squeeze all his body behind a little heap of flat stones. It didn't dawn upon him until the excitement had passed and the gunfire died away that his little stack of rocks wasn't a natural formation at all. He was lying atop an ancient Indian grave. He squirmed away and took cover in the prickly underbrush.

Brigham Pruett had recognized the lawmen, and now, stepping out into plain sight and starting on up the west slope, he said in a perfectly normal tone of voice: "Come on you two . . . there are still others up there."

Jess called after the burly, older man, but Pruett kept on walking, his smoky gaze riveted upon that yonder slope.

"Cover him," called Huff. "The damned fool. Those two'll abandon their horses and creep back. Cover him!"

Jess squirmed around until he had a good sighting along that west slope. He'd lost his hat in their downhill plunge and both boots were full of sand, but he got up onto one knee, shouldered his rifle, and fired into that clump where he and Fred Huff had been.

The Texan also fired uphill.

Whether it was this disconcerting rifle fire or whether it was simply the prudence inspired by seeing their companions killed, when Pruett reached the uphill lip, there were no horsemen visible out over the desert in any direction. He turned and gestured for Wright and Huff to come on up.

They went, trudging along side-by-side with nothing to

say until they got up where the saddle maker was standing, his mighty legs spread wide, his Winchester carbine cradled in his arms. Then Huff looked scathingly at the shock-headed big man and said: "A man can push his luck just so far, Pruett. I think you've pushed yours beyond the limit. What the hell were you thinking of, walkin' up this lousy hill standin' straight up?"

Pruett looked at Huff, and looked away. It was hot, the sun was reddening off in the hazy west, and Brigham Pruett's face was impassively and fatalistically set in an unbending expression. "How'd you get out of Singing Springs?" he asked Jess, ignoring the Texas Ranger completely.

"Side-riding on a couple of bareback horses in the midst of some of Sam Potts's loose stock," Jess answered. "Brigham, they've got Angela Miflin."

Pruett's head swung as though he'd been slapped. His eyes acquired a bright, hard light to them. He kept staring at Jess. "How?" he asked.

"Shad Adams went out alone. She saw him leavin' town, saddled her damned horse, and went after him."

"I see. And Adams . . . ?"

Jess lifted his shoulders and dropped them. "We thought you might've seen him out here somewhere."

"No. I've been stalkin' the others."

"You were behind the ones that came up from the south," put in Fred Huff. "We caught a reflection of sunlight off your gun barrel."

"I didn't want them," said Pruett stonily. "I want the Wiltons. I want one Wilton particularly."

Fred Huff was balancing something in his mind, but he never said it, whatever it was. He simply dropped his glance to the ground for a solemn moment, then swung his head to gaze around. There was no sign of those two outlaws who had escaped. Fred struck at the dust on his trousers, and swung half around from the waist to gaze over where those two patiently standing horses were still tied beyond the north rim. As he swung back, he said: "Pruett, where's your horse?"

"Down in the arroyo near the east spring. Why?"

"Go get him. The three of us together can do a lot more than any one of us can do alone."

"No. I'll stay to m'self, Ranger."

Huff's glare flamed. "You figure your private feud's more important than keepin' the Wiltons from killin' that girl?"

"They won't kill her, Ranger," growled the saddle maker.

Jess fished in a pocket, brought out a limp scrap of paper, and wordlessly pushed it at Pruett, who took it, read it, re-read it, and handed it back, his expression changing a little, turning still grimmer and more cruel. He started to move away.

"I'll fetch my horse an' meet you boys atop the north rim."

After Pruett had departed, Jess and Fred Huff started on across the desert floor toward the two tethered horses. Twice, Jess tried to strike up a conversation, and both times the Ranger ignored him as though he didn't even know Wright was around. Clearly Fred Huff had something on his mind which was foreign to all this, and just as clearly he had no intention of mentioning it.

They came upon the dead man who had dropped like a stone at the first volley and saw instantly why he'd done that. Huff's slug had struck him directly between the eyes.

They went on past, got the two tethered horses, tested *cinchas,* adjusted stirrups, and swung up. Moments later, when Brigham Pruett came up, he'd evidently been thinking of all that had thus far happened because, as he eased over beside Jess, he said: "Yesterday I didn't dare tell you I was going to try and get the Wiltons alone, Jess. If I had, you'd have probably thrown down on me."

Jess inclined his head. "I would have," he conceded. "But that's all behind us now."

They looked. There were three converging columns of rising dust heading straight toward their arroyo, and one of them was fanning up from the southeast. Fred straightened around, gazed on over toward the broken, twisted badlands, and said: "No other choice, boys. Let's go."

They broke into a gallop without any further talk. Those converging riders were undoubtedly the spying segments of the Wilton crowd, and just as obviously those two men who had witnessed the fight at the arroyo and had afterward raced away had somehow managed to signal to all their other companions to hasten up.

Jess tried to guess what the odds would be now, but gave that up when he arrived at the approximate figure of three to one.

They swung down into the broken fissures of land by way of an ancient trail, and here Fred Huff, in the lead, craned around for directions. He didn't know these breaks at all. Pruett gestured east with his upraised carbine. Huff dutifully swung his mount off in that direction, and the three of them went twisting and turning in and out of erosion gulches sometimes ten feet deep, sometimes thirty feet deep, but always narrow and always shadowed by high-standing spirals of twisted, tortured sandstone rising up on both sides in every conceivable shape.

It was now close to six o'clock.

When Fred finally set his horse up in a long slide because dead ahead of him was the sheer bluff face of a blind cañon, Jess slowed to get his bearings. He knew these breaks, had, in fact, hunted among them for deer and smaller game many times.

"Follow me!" he called to the others, reversed his horse, and went at a fast trot back to where they'd entered the blind cañon, then swung off eastward again, and kept on a crooked, angling course that eventually led them around the brushy base of a perfectly level small overhead plateau. Here, with one man atop the flat to watch and the other two men down below armed and ready, they could hold off an army.

"Until," as Jess said, "our ammunition runs out . . . and, after that, if we can't sprout wings, we're goners."

Pruett started to climb up to the tabletop of gravelly land, but Ranger Huff called over to him: "Pruett, you stay down here with me for now. Let Jess take the first watch."

Pruett craned around and didn't move or speak for a long while, or until he'd made up his mind to comply. Afterward, as Jess took Pruett's place climbing up to their sentinel spot, he thought privately that Huff hadn't just given that order because he thought Brigham needed the rest. Huff had something to say to Pruett he didn't want anyone else to hear.

From his vantage point Jess had a good view of the surrounding broken, slashed, and deeply cut-up roundabout countryside. Their horses badly needed rest. It was a killing pace, running horses in this kind of weather. But now the animals would get their respite, for although Jess saw those dust clouds yonder leave the area of the arroyo heading into the badlands, with the pre-evening shadows coming it would take a lot of time and a lot of luck for the Wiltons to find Jess and Huff and burly Brigham Pruett.

Down below in the humid hush Jess heard Pruett's rumbling bull-bass voice, and he also heard Fred Huff speaking. It seemed that Huff was doing most of the talking, that Pruett was only hollowly assenting from time to time.

The outlaws came right up to the edge of the badlands and halted. Jess could see them, small in the westerly distance.

They had trailed their prey without any difficulty that far, but now it seemed to Jess that there was dissension among them as to how they should proceed.

Finally the band started moving again, and Jess was surprised, and made uneasy, for the renegades were not going down into the maze work of gullies and arroyos and blind-cañon gulches, which he'd been confident they'd do in order to track Jess and his companions. They were instead fanning out in a big surround whose obvious and only purpose could be to seal off this limited stretch of wild country so that the wanted lawmen and their companion from Singing Springs could not get out alive.

Where, he wondered, would a man learn that kind of strategy? Every outlaw band he'd ever encountered went straight after an enemy. This, he thought, was too much like an army maneuver. He went to the edge of their table top and dropped straight down to land within twenty feet of Huff and Pruett, both solemnly silent now and sitting like statues.

Jess explained what the Wiltons were up to. Huff listened with close interest, but Brigham Pruett's hazy eyes began to sharpen with quick, hard interest. It was almost as though what Jess was saying pleased the saddle maker, and, when Jess ceased speaking, Pruett said: "It's nothing really new, Sheriff, an' like all strategy, there's a counter-measure to be used against it."

Jess gazed at the saddle maker. Beside Pruett the Texas Ranger got an ironic look around his eyes. He said to Jess: "Better let the saddle maker take over from here on, Sheriff."

Huff made that statement with full confidence in his voice, but, when Jess gazed straight at him, Huff simply rolled his head gently from side to side. He was not going to elaborate.

Pruett stood up, shot a glance skyward as though estimating the time, then he scooped up his leaning carbine and stepped over where their recovered horses stood drowsing.

"We leave the animals," he said to Jess. "Unsaddle them. It's the humane way."

Jess started to protest, but Huff looked straight at him, shaking his head again in that same fully confident, ironic manner. Jess shrugged. He went over and off-saddled, off-bridled, then waited.

Pruett stepped back, and turned with a jerk of his head. "Come along. We couldn't even hope to get through mounted, but on foot we can." He looked back, saw Jess's troubled expression, and added: "Don't worry. We'll get three more horses just like you and the Ranger got those two you rode here. Now come along . . . and don't make a sound."

As Jess came even with Huff, the Ranger looked up, his perpetually squinted eyes like bright chips of steel. In a tone so low Pruett, who was several hundred feet ahead, could not hear, he said: "Sheriff, I reckon you've been wondering. Well, you got a right to, an' maybe when this is all over I'll tell you . . . but right now just put your faith in Brig Pruett and don't ask any questions."

Jess nodded. "I'll keep the questions to myself," he agreed. "I could hear you two talkin' down below me, back there where we left the horses. But before that I had a feeling, too . . . well, let's forget personalities right now. What's worrying me is where they've got Angela Miflin."

"With them," stated the Ranger. "Where else? They wouldn't dare leave her unguarded some place out on this lousy desert, and they wouldn't take a chance on leavin' one or two men to guard her. I'll stake my reputation that wherever Frank Wilton is right now, Miss Miflin isn't more'n arm's distance away."

"I sure hope you're right, Ranger," breathed Jess.

Huff hiked along for a minute or two, then he said: "It's

Shad Adams I'm wondering about. You know, Sheriff, he's no fool, and he's been out of sight of everyone for a long time. Now, I know Shad pretty well. This isn't like him. I'll bet cash money he's up to something. Don't ask me what because I've got no idea under the sun, but. . . ." Huff stopped speaking at a curt sign from Pruett up ahead, stepped carefully along in total silence until he and Jess came up even with the saddle maker, who had stopped to listen, and the three of them afterward melted back into long shadows while the oncoming sounds of a walking horse sounded overhead, up along the ragged lip of the broken country.

The sun was dropping down fast now. There was a quiet, red hotness to the desert. Down in the breaks, though, where shade had been strongly evident for several hours, it was cooler, and occasionally a trapped little hot breeze would scuttle around through the arroyos bringing a particularly refreshing kind of acrid-scented wind to dry sweat from the three stalking men.

Northward a coyote suddenly yapped in frantic excitement, evidently routed out of his daytime hideaway by the approach of one of the circling horsemen. Jess braced, expecting a gunshot over this meeting of ancient enemies, but none came. Apparently Frank Wilton had passed an order there was to be no shooting unless the men from Singing Springs were located.

The long shadow of a silent horseman passed over the place where the lawmen and Brigham Pruett stood, scarcely breathing, then it was gone, and Pruett turned with a gesture, moving out westerly again. Jess made a mocking gesture of wiping sweat off his forehead as he and Huff stepped forth into the saddle maker's wake again. That had been a close call.

Chapter Seventeen

Pruett's strategy was elemental enough. He meant to sneak through that surround on foot, which he did, leading his companions silently through the friendly shadows. But until they were up against the same westerly breaks where they'd initially gone down into the broken country, Jess hadn't understood exactly what the saddle maker was up to.

Now he did, though, as they came at long last to a stealthy halt beside the same identical game trail they'd used to get down into the breaks, and Pruett held a thick finger across his pursed lips as he intently listened, straining to pick up any sign above them on the desert.

But the yonder world was as deathlessly silent as it always seemed to be near the end of the hot summertime days, so Pruett lowered his hand, drew out his .45, and dipped its heavy barrel up and down. "Don't fire unless you absolutely have to. Try to get the drop or hit them from behind, but don't shoot. One gunshot, and they'll converge on us like wolves." Pruett paused to gaze over at Fred Huff, then he said: "It doesn't matter who we are or who they are. If they catch us, they'll kill on sight. Now, follow me. We'll creep up onto the desert floor and head around from west to north. What we need now is three horses . . . and little Angie. Be careful an' be quiet. Let's go."

It was surprisingly easy. There were no mounted outlaws close by, and even though it was beginning to turn shadowy over the desert, there was still enough light to see a fair distance by.

Pruett slashed with a thick arm and dropped down. Jess and Huff did the same. There was a rider passing along toward them from the east. This man was probably the same rider they'd hidden from earlier along the same eastern rampart.

They watched the man come. There was a fringe of scraggly brush back a short distance that they crawled behind and waited. The horseman was young and dissipated-looking. He was dirty, unshaven, and cruel-mouthed, and, although he kept his dutiful vigil, he was watching in the wrong direction, down into the badlands nearest him.

Once he paused to whittle off a chew of tobacco, pouch it in his left cheek, return the plug to his shirt pocket, and pick up his reins again. There was something about this outlaw that left a definite impression upon people, even when they had never seen him before and first viewed him. Fred Huff formed it into one word with his lips, but he didn't say it aloud: *Killer.*

He was a much younger man than Fred, but he was the same in height and build, and he had the double rig, the duck-bill low horn, and the A-fork cut to his saddle that said Texas as far off as his outfit could be seen.

Pruett, silent all through the moment their enemy was taking his chaw and wearily gazing over into the twisted, dark, and dusty breaks, finally made his decision and his move. He stood straight up with his carbine held two-handed across his lower body and said: "Don't move!"

The renegade gave a little swift jerk of astonishment, then very slowly rolled his head around to where he could see Pruett. His heretofore masticating jaws were entirely still. He and the saddle maker exchanged a long, long look. Pruett was waiting for the younger man to make up his mind. The gunman was estimating his chances.

174

When Jess and Fred Huff rose up silently on each side of Pruett, the outlaw had his mind made up for him. He began rhythmically ruminating again, spat amber, and said: "All right, fellers, you win. Hey, Huff, how'd you get here?"

"Flew," growled the Ranger. "Go on over and disarm him, Pruett. Stay off to one side."

The outlaw made no attempt to move, allowed himself to be disarmed, and continued his chewing and his steady appraisal of the Ranger, a sulphurous yet seemingly impersonal appraisal.

"Get off the horse!" Huff ordered. The outlaw stepped obediently down, hooked his thumbs in his belt, and kept staring unblinkingly at the Texan.

"Huff, they got a five thousand dollar reward on your topknot now. Not dead or alive . . . just dead."

"You'll never collect it," Huff snapped. "Pruett," said the Ranger, and coldly inclined his head. They all knew what Huff meant, even the youthful killer, but he, least of all, did anything about it, and, when Pruett crunched his pistol barrel down across the killer's head, dropping him in his tracks, right up until unconsciousness came the gunman went on brightly staring and masticating.

Huff put up his gun, never once taking his eyes off the downed man. "Use his belts to lash his ankles and his arms, Brigham, an', if you don't do it right an' this one gets loose, we'll never catch him like this again."

Jess watched the saddle maker go to work. He stepped across, took the horse's reins to keep the beast from wandering off, examined the outlaw's Winchester, and tossed it aside. His own rifle was much better.

Huff came over. "You're wondering," he said, jerking a thumb downward. "His name's Muley Perkins. He's been with the Wiltons two years now. He's a Texas boy. In fact,

Muley comes from the same town I do, an' his pappy was a friend of mine for many years. Muley's worth two thousand dollars dead or alive. He's the one I told you about Shad Adams havin' a little brush with one time. He's a murderer, a thief, a liar, and just about anything else you want to call him."

Brigham Pruett completed the tying and stood up, examining his work. It was well done, Jess thought, seeing the way those belts had been twisted and cinched up. Sometime during his life Pruett had learned to do this kind of work very well.

"I'll take the horse and go get us another one," Pruett said, stepping unconcernedly across the outlaw's trussed body, but Huff shook his head.

"We'll tie the critter back a ways and *all* go, Brigham."

Jess led the horse and secured him beyond sight. When he returned, Pruett and Huff were talking. They broke it off abruptly when Jess came up, and, as though they hadn't been discussing anything private, the Ranger said he thought Jess, who knew this country, should lead in search of their next mount.

Jess did, but instead of heading on around easterly, he went north. There was much better cover in this direction, but more than anything else it was in his mind that, if they came up on more outlaws, they'd be behind them, and, if they were heard or sighted, when the outlaws turned to face them, they'd have that red blaze of setting sun in their eyes. When a man was laying his life on the line, he accumulated every advantage he could.

They came around through the buck brush, the sage, and spiny chaparral twisting and turning, with the strong scent of horse sweat in their nostrils, but actually, despite their suspicions and their efforts, they did not spy the cause of this odor until where an erosion gully sixty or seventy feet deep and straight down cut back a half mile or so straight northward. There, less than a hundred feet away, they saw two men sitting atop their mounts idly talking and smoking.

At once the three of them dropped down.

This was not a good thing, though. Between their buck brush patch and the bored outlaws was at least forty feet of sheer tan desert without any cover upon it of any kind, and, because one of those men was facing the squattier of that pair, whose back was to the fugitives, he commanded an excellent rearward view, making it wholly impossible for the men from Singing Springs to get up close without detection.

"Shoot," whispered Pruett, then, as soon as the others also decided this would be the only way, Pruett suddenly pushed down their gun barrels. "No, there's another way. Cover me."

Neither Huff nor Jess Wright had a chance to remonstrate or reach out before the burly saddle maker dropped his carbine, shed his .45, and stood straight up. Jess, who was in a position to observe it, saw that farthest outlaw's eye spring wide open as his whisker-stubbled jaw sagged in purest astonishment.

"I quit," said Pruett, making his voice unsteady, making it quaver as he stepped, loose-jointed, out of the brush. "Broke my carbine back in the arroyo and lost m'damned pistol crawlin' up out of these lousy breaks. I quit."

The outlaw with his back to Pruett unhooked his right leg and dropped to the ground, twisting around as he did so. The other man had his gun palmed and pointed but neglected to cock it, a fatal mistake any time.

It obviously was this totally unexpected appearance even more than Pruett's pretense of exhaustion and demoralization that kept those two renegades speechless until the powerfully compact saddle maker got right up beside the dismounted man.

"Those other two . . . they're still down in the breaks, but one's got a hurt ankle where his horse fell with him and the other one . . . that Texas lawman . . . he's out of ammunition after the fight over in the arroyo."

Finally the mounted outlaw unwound and lit down beside his companion. He made a curt gesture, saying to his partner: "Search him, Bert, then let's get t'hell over where Frank is. Remember what he said about a thousand for bringin' any one of 'em in . . . well . . . here's five hundred apiece, an' maybe we'll pick up another pocketful when we shed this here one."

The renegade called Bert stepped up behind Brigham Pruett and roughly ran his hands up and down. "Nothin'," he said, moving around where he'd have a closer look at the saddle maker. "This ain't the one that killed Johnny," he mumbled, "an' he sure don't answer the description of that Ranger, so I reckon this one's tellin' the truth."

The outlaw with the gun had his back to Jess and Fred Huff. That was no accident. Pruett had stopped and turned so that his captor would have to stand like that to face him.

The nearest outlaw, with his face screwed up, stepped back a little and tilted his head to make a close study of his prisoner. He had his hand on his holstered .45. Sharply and very clearly a man's voice spoke up from forty feet off, turning this man suddenly to stone.

"Freeze, both of you. Make one move and it'll be the last you ever make."

"Tricked," snarled the outlaw with the drawn gun, and spun around, but he'd sealed his own doom moments before by drawing that gun and neglecting to cock it. Brigham Pruett sprang flat-footed, struck the whirling man with a pile-driving shoulder, crashed to the ground with him, and both of them threshed frantically seeking control of the gun. The outlaw did not relinquish his hold, but Pruett's powerful grip on the man's wrist as they rolled forced the gun downward and inward. When it exploded, the outlaw was lying atop it. He gave a violent upward spring that carried them both six inches off the ground, then he turned all limp and loose, dead from his own gun and by his own hand. Pruett rolled aside, got up onto one knee, gazed at the dead man's twisted face, and looked away.

Huff and Jess Wright had the other outlaw under their guns. Only a complete fool would have tried to draw against a drop.

Jess disarmed this man, but as he was stepping back, the renegade, probably realizing that his own demise was certain if he allowed himself to be taken back to Singing Springs, dropped down and whirled, driving straight for the sheriff. Jess could not fire. Brigham Pruett was directly behind the outlaw, and Fred Huff was on his immediate right. He swung his gun overhand and missed as the outlaw hit him, flailing at his face and head with both fists.

Jess turned away from that wild punishment, flung aside his pistol, turned back, and braced himself into the fierce attack. He struck the desperate man over the heart, driving him off. He struck him alongside the jaw, making him stagger, and, when the outlaw spun unsteadily as though to rush for his horse, Jess dug in his heels, sprang ahead, caught the man's left shoulder, and spun him around. This time he hit him flush in the mouth, driving the outlaw's head back so violently his hat sailed off five feet and dropped straight downwards.

One moment his adversary was recoiling from that blow, the next moment neither he nor his hat were in front of Jess at all. The sheriff'd had no idea how close they'd fought to the sheer drop-off into the gully below. Now, seeing that dark and gloomy slot open at his feet, he dropped both arms and stared. Sixty or seventy feet below lay the outlaw. He'd landed on his head and shoulders, lying relaxed down there in the gathering gloom with his head at a sickening angle.

"Broke his neck," breathed Fred Huff, peering downward as he put up his gun and halted beside Jess. "He didn't feel it, though. That last punch knocked him out." Huff looked around, then gruffly said: "Come on, Jess. Forget it. You didn't plan it that way."

Pruett was gazing at the other man. As Jess and Huff moved away from the crumbly sheer bank, Pruett turned swiftly and scowled. "Riders," he said crisply. "They must've heard the shot when this one fell on his gun an' it went off. We got to get out of here."

Huff and Jess also heard the oncoming men. Huff gestured swiftly toward the saddled horses and began moving away even as he said: "Get aboard, you two, and come on." Huff went running swiftly back through the brush down toward where they'd left the third saddled animal. Behind him Jess and Brigham Pruett piled across leather, whirled, and lit out. They didn't pass Fred. They didn't even catch up to him until they were more than halfway back down country the way they'd earlier stalked up northward. They remained a short distance behind Huff all the way back to the horse, just in case, but the alerted outlaws didn't show up. They had evidently been stopped by the sight of that dead man up there, lying atop his own gun.

The sun was nearly gone now. Shadows were banked in layers atop the desert floor. Where the brush was thickest, the shadows were also thickest.

Huff was out of wind by the time he got to that tethered

horse, shoved his rifle into the empty saddle boot, untied the animal, and got gratefully astride. He let Jess and Pruett come alongside, then he pantingly said: "We'll never make it back to town now. Lead out, Jess. We got a fight on our hands!"

Chapter Eighteen

There was only one place for three desperate men to go—the arroyo. Jess roweled his horse, and with Fred Huff being trailed by big Brigham Pruett the three of them careened due southward.

Evening was closing in, which was definitely in their favor. They could distinctly make out the reverberations of the Wiltons, pressing swiftly down country in their wake, and this was just as definitely *not* in their favor.

Jess didn't slacken his gait as he came to the downward slope into the arroyo. Brigham Pruett tried to slow his excited mount, but the beast had a mouth of iron. It resisted all Pruett's efforts and went recklessly plunging downhill, overtaking and nearly running over Ranger Huff.

They got down into the paloverdes, hit the ground with rifles and carbines in hand, and started to scatter for cover. A man appeared out of the underbrush calling to them to wait, to hold up, and not to shoot. It was Shad Adams.

Jess skidded to a halt as he recognized the younger man. So did Huff and Pruett, but what held the three of them totally speechless wasn't Shad Adams, it was Angie Miflin there in the gloomy shadows behind Adams. She looked sun-scorched and upset, but otherwise unharmed.

"They're comin' right behind us," snarled Jess, beginning to move again.

Adams stepped forth with a flinty gaze upward along the north rim. "Let 'em come," he growled. He twisted and made a motion with one hand. Out of the rearward brush arose Pete

Odell, Charley Miflin, Sam Potts, and Buster Hilton, all with carbines in hand.

This time, as Jess halted, Brigham Pruett let off a mild oath of astonishment. "How the hell . . . what are you fellers doing here?"

Swarthy Buster Hilton said: "The same thing you are, Pruett . . . come out to settle the hash for the Wiltons."

"But how . . . ?"

"Adams. He signaled from out here with a mirror Angie had in her pocket. Sam could read Morse code and, well, we come on out all together, Wiltons or no Wiltons."

Fred Huff twisted to look anxiously up along the north rim. "No time for talk now!" he exclaimed. "Get to cover. They'll bust over that rim in less than a minute."

The underbrush wasn't as thick down in the arroyo as it had been up on the floor of the desert, but down here there were spidery little green-trunked paloverde trees, and, more favorably, there were darker shadows because this place was well below the reach of the failing daylight.

Jess got into cover beside Shad Adams. Charley Miflin, obviously released from jail by the others, took his daughter away from the others, seeking better protection for her.

"How'd you get her?" Jess asked, standing up to lay his rifle in the crotch of a little paloverde. "We thought she was still with the Wiltons."

"She was, until about two hours ago," Adams said. "A couple of their men came up, saying something about there being some men from town around here where they'd gotten out of town on loose horses. Frank and the others went hell for leather to see about that. Lance was left to fetch Angie along. I was on foot in the sage when Lance started out. I gave him one chance to quit, then I shot him. It was his horse I used to get here, with Angie. That's when I signaled for help with her little glass mirror."

Brigham Pruett's bull-bass voice drowned out every other sound as eight riders or so appeared on the north rim, guns up and swinging.

"Frank!" called Pruett. "Frank, don't go any further with this."

A thick-shouldered, shock-headed, fair-complexioned big man astride a fine black gelding drew and fired at the sound of Pruett's voice. All along the rim guns flashed red and shattered the breathless hush with their bucking thunder.

Out of the underbrush around Jess guns exploded.

Atop the rim three saddles were emptied in that first volley from the townsmen. It was an unprecedented feat, firing uphill at moving, milling targets in the lengthening gloom of evening. One of those astonished outlaws up above gave a shout of dismay, whirled his horse, and fled. His companions, though, fired straight back down into the arroyo.

Jess felt a bullet tug at his baggy shirt. He heard the cloth rip. He fired at one of the mounted men and missed.

Pruett cried out again, this time with anguish and desperation in his voice. "Frank . . . stop. You're skylined. *Stop!*"

But the rider of that handsome black horse waved his six-gun around his head, set his horse to the downhill slope, and mercilessly spurred the big beast. Around Frank Wilton the other renegades broke out into the same downhill charge.

Now the gunfire around Jess became deafening as his companions, on foot, realized their plight. Unless they broke up that charge before those horsemen reached them, they would be flushed out into the open and shot down.

Fred Huff sprang up from behind a bush and blazed away in a crouched, gunfighting stance.

Brigham Pruett did a desperate thing. He got upright, took several forward steps as though seeking to distract the horsemen, as though he meant to draw them toward him, which is what happened, and he fired from the hip as he took each onward step. It was suicide.

Jess, his eyes stinging from burned powder, emptied a saddle with his rifle, then abandoned it, and drew his .45. The fight swirled up very close now, but there were more riderless, panicked horses coming at the battlers on the ground than there were ridden animals. The decimation had been terrible.

Charley Miflin and Pete Odell, far back, were kneeling side-by-side with their shouldered carbines blazing. Swarthy, battle-scarred Buster Hilton fired and roared defiant curses at the same time.

Jess saw that burly man on the black gelding loom up, his gun redly flashing. He winced from a near miss and swung to fire. His six-gun was empty. He had a perfect look at the outlaw leader's contorted, cruel face, then suddenly the black horse gave a tremendous bound forward as though creased by a stinging bullet, struck Jess, and knocked him down. As he rolled clear and got up on one knee, he saw the black horse plunge past, riderless.

Two men were on foot out where the attackers had been. One was seeking desperately to reach the shelter of a distant sage clump; the other one was out there, wide-legged and savagely defiant. Ironically enough, the fleeing desperado, who was not firing his gun, was hit first. He went down in a headlong dive. The other man, hit hard, sank to his knees, but he kept on firing until his gun was empty. Then he took several more hard hits, and eased over slowly to land face down upon the churned earth.

Shad Adams and a stocky man were on the ground rolling over and over, each trying to club the other over the head with an empty gun. Jess got to his feet, stepped over where those two were threshing, panting, and whipping this way and that, waited until the stocky man's head came up briefly out of the churning dust, and struck. The stocky man shuddered, his eyes rolled up aimlessly, and Shad pushed him off. He tumbled aside, broken and senseless. Shad got up onto his feet and aimed his empty gun at the man, held it like that for a moment, then flung the gun away as he turned, his lower lip bleeding, and said: "That's Stub Wilton. You shouldn't have interfered, Sheriff. I wanted that one dead, too."

The gunfire abruptly ended.

Jess twisted to gaze around. Fred Huff was sitting upon the ground with his legs thrust straight out in front of him, holding his left shoulder and rocking back and forth. Blood oozed past his fingers. Pete Odell came stiffly up with Charley Miflin, both of them breathing hard. There was one outlaw left. He was standing with both arms rigidly overhead, with his eyes full of shock and with his lips quivering. He seemed too stunned to speak or to move. He was the only member of the dreaded Wilton gang still on his feet.

Jess went over to where Fred was whispering grisly curses, knelt, and reached up to examine Huff's bloody shoulder.

The Ranger pulled back. "I'll live," he said, staring bitterly straight ahead. "Jess, Pruett's stopped the big six out there."

Jess turned to look, saw the saddle maker lying on his stomach with his head off the ground, and started to stand up.

"Listen," gasped Huff through clenched teeth. "That feller twenty feet beyond . . . that's Frank Wilton . . . he was ridin' the big black gelding. Listen, Sheriff, carry Pruett over to Frank and leave them together."

Jess looked baffled.

Huff, his pain intense, said: "Dammit, do like I say. Put

Pruett over by Frank and leave 'em. I'll explain later."

Jess walked on out where Brigham lay, saw the leaking claret from four fatal bullet holes, bent down without a word, got the saddle maker under the armpits, and half dragged, half carried him over to where the thick-shouldered dead outlaw leader lay. As he was easing Pruett down, he thought he heard him say: "Son . . . son."

Charley Miflin and Shad Adams walked up. Charley looked down and didn't say a word. Neither did Shad Adams. Pete Odell and Buster Hilton, supporting Fred Huff between them, came up and also gravely stopped to gaze earthward. Charley Miflin knelt over Brigham Pruett, smoothed back a tumbled, graying lock of the saddle maker's hair, bent lower still, and remained like that for a moment before he raised his eyes to the others and said: "He's dead. Brigham's dead."

"They're both dead," Fred Huff mumbled gruffly. "Anybody got a drink of whisky on 'em?" No one had. Huff let off a pent-up breath and said: "I didn't think so. It'd have made things easier is all . . . Jess?"

"Yeah?" said Sheriff Wright, looking around.

"You deserve some answers. Now I'll give 'em to you. You recollect me tellin' you that Alice Wilton married twice and got a fledgling gun hand along with her second husband?"

"I remember."

"Well, you're lookin' at him. Frank Wilton. What I *didn't* tell you, Sheriff, was her second husband's name . . . *Brigham Pruett!*"

Jess was stunned. So were the others standing there. For a while none of them said a word. When a man eventually did speak, it was Shad Adams.

"Any of you fellers see who shot Frank off his black horse?"

"Yeah," mumbled Huff. "The saddle maker of Singing

Springs did it. I saw it. Maybe the rest of you didn't understand what he was yellin' when those outlaws appeared on the rim up there. He was beggin' Frank not to make him do it." Huff shook his head. "He knew . . . the same as I knew . . . Frank would do it anyway."

Angela came walking forward. Shad saw her, stepped away from the others, went across to take her arm, and walked back away from the dead men with her.

Jess looked around. The others briefly met his glance but only briefly. This was an unnerving time for all of them. Finally Buster Hilton turned away, saying: "Come on, Pete. Sam's over in the brush with a slug through his leg. Let's help him get the thing bandaged, then round up the prisoners and fetch the horses up for the trip back."

When only the pair of them were left out in the sooty evening with Brigham Pruett and Frank Wilton, Huff said: "Sheriff, you maybe wondered where Frank got all his savvy . . . like surroundin' those badlands out there. Well, Brigham Pruett was one of Texas' most famous . . . or infamous, whichever you prefer . . . guerilla captains during the war. He told Frank a lot of stories when the boy was growing up."

"You recognized Pruett, Ranger?"

"Yeah, I recognized him, Sheriff. Recognized him my first day in Singing Springs. Tell you something else, too . . . he recognized me. Why'd you think he had that big glass window installed in his saddle shop? So's he could see the law before the law saw him. Maybe there was more to it than that, but, you see, Brigham Pruett was involved in sackin' and burnin' a Yankee town after the Confederate defeat at Gettysburg, and, when amnesty was granted after the war, well, Brigham Pruett was excluded because of that sacking. He went to Mexico one jump ahead of the Texas Rangers. Well, the war was a long time ago, an' Brigham Pruett paid for whatever he

188

did wrong a thousand times over in the years that followed. Lost his little girl, his wife . . . then this . . . died shooting it out with his own son."

Jess lifted his eyes to Huff's bronzed, grizzled face. "Just answer me one question, Ranger," he asked softly. "If Pruett had survived today . . . would you have taken him back to Texas?"

Huff's eyes flickered, then dropped. His thin-lipped, uncompromising mouth loosened. The hand holding his scarlet-stained shoulder briefly convulsed. "That's been in my mind ever since I hit your town," he said, "and thank God I don't have to answer it for you . . . or for myself. Not now. Come on, the others are over at the spring. Let's go."

Off in the faraway north a thin little silvery moon was floating through a rash of pewter stars. There was that night-time acrid desert dust odor in the still, hot air. No one had much to say as they tied the dead across their saddles, helped the injured astride, and tied the solitary surviving member of the notorious Wilton gang atop his horse.

Shad Adams and Angela Miflin rode off first, heading southeast in the direction of Singing Springs. An awful lot of hatred remained back in the quiet arroyo as the others also rode away, and, if the threads of many lives had worked toward their final unraveling in this out of the way place, perhaps it was, as Fred Huff told Jess Wright, proof that life isn't very strong, not even in the most dedicated of men.

"And one last thing," he murmured, as the two lawmen slouched along far back behind the others. They had to pick up Muley Perkins. "You and I can thank our stars for the fact that Singin' Springs turned out to be a place where old gunfighters and old outlaws went to live out their last years and to die, because if we'd had just ordinary men down there with us when the Wiltons charged off that rim, we'd never have left that arroyo alive."

"Outlaws?" said Jess. "Gunfighters?"

Huff lifted his gray face and softly smiled. "Well," he said. "Just between you 'n' me, you understand. I'd never write anythin' like that in a report. Every man livin' deserves his second chance, don't you agree?"

"Positively," said Jess, and looked far ahead where Angie and Shad Adams were riding. "Positively, Ranger, every man deserves his second chance."

BORDER TOWN
LAURAN PAINE

Nestled on the border of New Mexico since long before there was a New Mexico, the small town of San Ildefonso has survived a lot. Marauding Indians, bandoleros, soldiers in blue and raiders in rags have all come and gone. Yet the residents of San Ildefonso remain, poor but resilient.

But now renegades from south of the border are attempting to seize the town, in search of a rumored conquistador treasure. With few young men able to fight, the village women and even the priest take up arms. But will it be enough? Will the courageous townspeople survive to battle another day?

Lockwood
LAURAN PAINE

In the Wyoming town of Derby, Cuff Lockwood is wounded in a gunfight and has to stay long enough to recuperate . . . and meet the pretty widow Lady Barlow, owner of the Barlow ranch. The ranch is in need of a ramrod, but Lockwood refuses the job. After all, Wyoming isn't what he had in mind. But it looks like Fate—or someone else—doesn't want Lockwood to leave town. When he tries he's ambushed and forced to stay again. It seems to Lockwood like his journey's ending, but sometimes life leads you down trails you never expected. Some mighty dangerous trails.

___4906-6 $4.50 US/$5.50 CAN

LAURAN PAINE

THE KILLER GUN

It is no ordinary gun. It is specially designed to help its owner kill a man. George Mars has customized a Colt revolver so it will fire when it is on half cock, saving the time it takes to pull back the hammer before firing. But then the gun is stolen from Mars's shop. Mars has engraved his name on it but, as the weapon passes from hand to hand, owner to owner, killer to killer, his identity becomes as much of a mystery as why possession of the gun skews the odds in any duel. And the legend of the killer gun grows with each newly slain man.

___4875-2 $4.50 US/$5.50 CAN

Dorchester Publishing Co., Inc.
P.O. Box 6640
Wayne, PA 19087-8640

Please add $2.50 for shipping and handling for the first book and $.75 for each book thereafter. NY, NYC, and PA residents, please add appropriate sales tax. No cash, stamps, or C.O.D.s. All orders shipped within 6 weeks via postal service book rate. Canadian orders require $2.50 extra postage and must be paid in U.S. dollars through a U.S. banking facility.

Name_____
Address_____
City_____State_____Zip_____
I have enclosed $ _____ in payment for the checked book(s).
Payment <u>must</u> accompany all orders. ☐ Please send a free catalog.
      CHECK OUT OUR WEBSITE! www.dorchesterpub.com